FOREVER

Until she met the handsome staff psychiatrist, Bill Aden, Noni Brisbane had been content with her loveless marriage to Philip, a top-flight surgeon. Then, through Bill, she learned that real love was possible forever, despite tragedy and hardship.

Books by Patricia Robins
Published by The House of Ulverscroft:

FORSAKEN

Never before available in hardcover, this edition has been fully revised and rewritten by the author who is perhaps better known as *Claire Lorrimer*.

PATRICIA ROBINS

◆

FOREVER

Complete and Unabridged

ULVERSCROFT
Leicester

First published in Great Britain in 1991

First Large Print Edition
published 2000

British Library CIP Data

Robins, Patricia, *1921* –
Forever.—Large print ed.—
Ulverscroft large print series: romance
1. Love stories
2. Large type books
I. Title
823.9'14 [F]

ISBN 0–7089–4175–3

Published by
F. A. Thorpe (Publishing) Ltd.
Anstey, Leicestershire

Set by Words & Graphics Ltd.
Anstey, Leicestershire
Printed and bound in Great Britain by
T. J. International Ltd., Padstow, Cornwall

This book is printed on acid-free paper

1

'Hello, Noni. How was Eileen?'

'Eileen? Oh, fine. She sent her love . . . '

She looked at her husband and thought: *Is he being sarcastic? No, of course not . . . it's natural he should ask after Eileen. Did I sound surprised . . . ? This is hell. A guilty conscience . . .*

'Come over here where I can touch you!'

She shut the door behind her and wished the few yards between her and Philip's bed were a hundred. She needed time . . . time to sort out her emotions. Time to prepare her defences. Pity was at war with guilt.

His arm was outstretched, his long slender surgeon's hands held gracefully and appealingly towards her. She drew off her glove and put her hand in his.

'You're cold. Is it still snowing? What did you do with yourself in that god-forsaken village? I've missed you.'

Steeling herself, she bent and kissed him.

'I've missed you, too!'

Liar, liar. I never thought of him once. There was no time to think of anyone but Bill . . .

'Well, you're very quiet. You're wearing a new perfume . . . I like it.'

Was it true that blind people developed their senses to a degree people with sight could not even guess at? It hadn't taken Philip two minutes to notice the new perfume. What else would he notice? His hands were exploring her face.

'You have such a lovely skin. Sit down. Tell me all about everything. You've no idea how disgustingly bored I've been without your daily visits. I never realized I'd miss you so much!'

'Oh, Philip!' For a moment, she couldn't guard against the pity. He heard it at once and his voice rose harshly:

'I don't want you to be sorry for me. I just wanted you to know how bloody boring it is lying here.'

Guilt replaced the pity. It was the moment when she should say:

'I won't go away again!' But she couldn't utter the lie — she would go — she had to go.

'Well, what did you do with yourself? Tea parties at the W.I.?'

She tried to think of Eileen, her sister, married to a not very successful solicitor and living in a Berkshire village near Reading. What *did* Eileen do with herself? She must remember . . .

'Oh, we went for walks, played bridge. I helped look after Micky.'

'I can't think why she has to call that ch̶ by such a stupid name. What the hell's wrong with Michael?'

'You know Eileen!'

'I suppose he's as crazy about you as ever?'

For one terrible moment she thought Philip was referring to Bill. His words kept repeating themselves inside her head like a reverberating drum: *crazy about you, crazy about you, crazy about you*. Bill's last words when he saw her off at the station had been: 'Darling, I'm crazy about you!'

'Don't tell me the kid had forgotten you!'

She let out her breath. Philip meant Micky — Eileen's little boy who had always adored his Aunt Noni. She returned that love in full because Micky was the nearest she'd ever come to a child of her own.

Philip hadn't wanted a family; he was too busy with his fantastic climb up the ladder of success; too single-minded and ambitious. Clear thinking, egotistical as always, he'd said:

'It wouldn't be fair. After all, what time would I have for kids?'

Now that there was time — all the time in the world, *she* did not want children — not Philip's children.

a bit of

1 has taught him to say Aunt
. I can't think how anyone as
ileen can so easily adopt the
ngs of her suburban hus-

im!'

Philip laughed. It wasn't really a cruel
laugh — just scornful.

'Honestly, that's a bit weak, isn't it? I mean,
you'd have thought if she loved him, she'd
have wanted to help him up a rung, not step
down one herself.'

Noni had known for a long while Philip
was a snob. In a way, it was one of the reasons
which had prompted him to marry her.
Funny, really! Philip came from a working-
class background but he'd climbed out of it.
How he despised his origin. He had meant to
become one of the leading surgeons in the
country and he hadn't wanted to be
handicapped by a working-class wife when he
got to what he called 'the top'. He'd married
sensibly — not a girl from the aristocracy
who might have been too much for him to
handle, but one from 'the county' — well
educated at good private schools; used to
money and to entertaining on the kind of
level surgeons might be expected to entertain.

Was he in love with me? I'll never know.
Maybe Philip is the sort of man whose mind

will always control his heart; who could direct himself to falling in love with what he felt to be the 'right' girl.

Philip could never understand why Eileen married Sydney. The argument was worn out now — always following the same pattern of words.

'She loves him.'

'I don't see how she *could* love a man like that . . .'

'But, Philip, you don't choose whom you're going to fall in love with. It just happens.'

'That's nonsense. Surely everyone has a certain amount of self-control. After all, Eileen is nearly as attractive as you . . . she could have married half a dozen different men who . . .'

'But she fell in love with *Sydney*!'

His voice brought her back to the present.

'How's Sydney doing these days? Still stuck in his rut?'

'He's quite happy, Philip. He and Eileen adore each other and they adore Micky.'

Her voice had risen. Philip noticed it at once.

'All right, calm down. If you must be so intense about them, at least spare me the details.'

'But, Philip, you asked . . .'

'I know. I'm sorry!' His hand was reaching

for hers again. She was trembling. If he noticed, he said nothing. He ran his fingers over the tips of her nails and said:

'You've broken one. What colour nail varnish have you got on? Have you changed that, too? I wish you wouldn't change things. It makes it more difficult for me.'

His voice was matter of fact but again, pity charged through her body like an overdose of adrenalin.

Of all people, Philip . . . blind! To be rendered so suddenly, so completely and so irrevocably helpless. Philip, who had treble the ordinary man's ambition; who couldn't stand being dependent; who had nothing else *but* his work — and to lose it at the very peak of success . . . Nothing else? The eye specialist, Harvey, had said:

'He's lucky to have you. In time, he'll accept the end of his career. You'll have to make a new life for him . . . have a family, perhaps? That would give him a new interest . . .'

But she'd been on the point of leaving Philip . . . of running away with Bill. How could she build a new life for Philip when, for over a year now, she'd been using all her energies to plan a new life for herself with Bill.

'Harvey says I'll have to stay in this

damned hospital at least another month. I wish to God I could come home. Well I'm going to insist I do go home before I'm forced into that damned rehabilitation centre.'

'Yes, of course, Philip. I'm sure Harvey will agree . . . '

'He'll damn well have to. This is a free country and once I'm discharged from here, I can do as I please. If I don't wish to, no one can force me to be *rehabilitated*.'

His voice was bitter. Noni tried very hard not to feel relieved because he was thinking now about himself and this stopped him asking questions about Eileen. She ought to have seen Eileen if only for a few minutes. She'd meant to that last morning but Bill had said:

'Darling, do you *have* to go? We could have another three hours — three hours . . . '

Eileen had seemed so unimportant with Bill's lips against hers. One would have thought that three days of kissing would have been sufficient. Bill had worked it out, his eyes laughing down at her: *'Seventy-two hours with an average of six kisses an hour comes to four hundred and thirty-two kisses. Is your mouth sore, my love?'*

'There could never be too many . . . Oh, Bill . . . '

'I hear Bill Aden is ill!'

'Bill?' Had she spoken the word aloud? How could he be ill? Oh, thank God Philip couldn't see her face! No, that was a terrible thought . . .

'Yes, Bill Aden, the consultant psychiatrist. He's been off with gastric 'flu. Harvey was telling me quite a few of the staff are down with it. Simcox and Parslow and half a dozen nurses.'

'I'm sorry. I hope it doesn't spread round the hospital.'

So that was how Bill had managed to get away! She'd forgotten to ask him. No, not forgotten, there just hadn't been time.

'Harvey's been pretty good — he comes in for a chat most afternoons; keeps me in touch. They . . . they've got a new man from Edinburgh in my place. Harvey says he's shaping quite well.'

This was Philip at his best — not bitter as he might have been about the man who'd stepped into his shoes. He had courage. How could one hit a man who'd been hit so hard already? It wasn't even as if the accident had been his fault. A foggy night and some stupid teenager showing off to his girl on the M.1. The boy had been killed outright and the girl, too. Only Philip had lived — to face the consequences. And her . . . and Bill . . .

'My love, I'm not going to ask you to leave him now. I know you wouldn't . . . and I wouldn't want you to. But when he's on his feet again, then you've got to do it; not just for yourself or for me, but for him. Pity is a terrible thing to live with — it'll destroy him.'

Was Bill speaking as a psychiatrist — or as a lover? How could she be sure? How could *Bill* be sure? Harvey had said just the opposite. Eileen had written:

'Of course, you won't be able to leave him and marry Bill now. I feel so heart-broken for you, darling. If there is anything I can do at any time to help, you know I will . . .'

Poor Eileen — she probably hadn't known then that she'd be called on to live up to her promise. She could help — by covering for her sister when she met Bill.

'Eileen, I can't live without seeing him. It isn't just sex although I'll admit that plays quite a large part. But I really love him, and he loves me. I know I can't leave Philip now but I have a right to some happiness. I'm asking you to cover for me not for my sake, or Bill's, but for Philip. He's the only one who'd be hurt if the truth came out. Please help us. You said you would.'

Eileen's letter had come by return of post.

'You can count on me. I'm afraid Sydney doesn't approve — one can hardly expect him to, I suppose, but he says he'll co-operate for my sake. I had to tell him because he might be the one to answer the phone or something. He says I'm to warn you that the whole situation is very risky indeed. Any court would be prejudiced against you when they learned of poor Philip's condition and you would both have to move. Could Bill find another job in another hospital? . . . '

Noni showed it to Bill.
'You let me worry about that, darling. Do you think I wouldn't risk a thousand jobs if I could live with you all the time? I'm young, strong and healthy. If the worst came to the worst, I could become a brick-layer. How'd you like that? Just feel those muscles on my shoulders . . . '
But her arms had not stayed around his shoulders and their conversation, like so many others, had ended in a tangled heap of discarded clothes upon the bedroom floor.
'I've told Harvey that if I don't get home soon, I'll go raving mad. I hate this place now.'

Poor Philip. Poor, poor Philip!

'And it isn't just being reminded all the bloody day about the career I've lost. I'm sick to death of lying here with nothing to do but listen to that blasted radio. If I was at home, at least I could make love to you. Do you realize that it's over two months since . . . '

Oh, no, Philip, I couldn't, I wouldn't want to. It's all different now . . . now there's Bill and I couldn't...

' . . . it would make me feel less cut off from everyone. God knows I never realized before what blind people have to endure. You feel you're missing something all the time. Now, for instance, I can't see your face. Have you got that shy-little-girl look you always adopt when I mention sex? Are you blushing? It never failed to stagger me the way you turned pink and looked like an embarrassed schoolgirl when I mentioned the topic of bed.'

Dear God, don't let him touch my face — he'll feel that I am trembling. Did he never realize that crude sex always disgusted me? One would have thought that a medical man would have known better.

Even after years she could still remember the shock of her wedding night. Partly because she was still very young — just eighteen — and partly because she'd had no

11

mother to guide and instruct her, she'd been extraordinarily ignorant and innocent. If Philip had been gentle and understanding — but he had been concerned only in claiming his 'rights' and had refused to curb his impatience to possess her, telling her:

'You'll enjoy it when you get used to it, Noni!'

Now, since Bill, she'd understood why it had all gone so wrong. Philip had been totally lacking in the one vital requirement, tenderness. It was an emotion he despised, for to him it meant weakness. He had not meant to be unkind. He truly believed that a woman appreciated domination in bed if not always out of it. On one of the rare occasions when he had been willing to discuss their unsatisfactory sex life he'd expressed his views quite openly and, so he believed, clinched his argument by quoting his past experiences with some of the nurses.

For a long, long time — until Bill, she'd believed that she was at fault. Philip was ten years older than she and in the medical profession. Surely he should know. She felt herself lacking in the proper feminine responses and accepted Philip's view that she was frigid. She'd even shyly warned Bill of her inadequacies and he had burst out laughing.

'You — frigid. Oh, Noni!'

She could smile about it now, too. With Bill. But she knew she could never share a bed with Philip again.

Now Philip said:

'You must be wanting it, too, after all this time. Never mind, darling, it won't be long now. What *is* that perfume you're wearing? It's beginning to turn me on. Well, at least that part of me isn't impaired. I suppose I should thank God for small mercies.'

'*If you could have chosen . . . your career or your ability to love a woman, which would you have chosen?*' she asked him silently.

'You're damn quiet. Nothing wrong?'

'I was just wondering, Philip . . . I was wondering whether if you could have chosen beforehand either to be made blind in the accident, or impotent, which you would have thought less terrible.'

He gave a sudden, unexpected laugh.

'You do think up some extraordinary things. As a matter of fact, it would be quite a puzzler. After all, my career as a surgeon could have gone on until I was seventy at least. On the other hand one could hope to go on satisfying one's desires for the same length of time.' He gave another laugh and patted her hand. 'Well, I don't suppose you'd have much difficulty if the choice were up to you — you'd rather I was blind, eh?'

How can men be so conceited? How can he have thought I ever really liked it. Oh, no, that isn't fair. Be honest! There were times, just occasionally, when she had wanted it in the same way as Philip — to satisfy an appetite. But mostly not in that way. Deep down she'd wished sex to be part of loving, and it had never been like that with Philip. With Bill, for the first time, she'd found that it could be so. Maybe all over the world there were women lying naked beneath their men, ignorant of this fact. Poor women . . . poor lonely, unhappy women married to men who did not know how to love.

'Funny thing about being blind . . . it gives your other senses an extra charge. Yesterday, Sister — Bristow is her name — came in with a message from Harvey. I never really noticed her before and then, suddenly, I heard her voice. Sexy wasn't in it — she was *asking* for it. Don't get me wrong, my dear. I wasn't in the least interested — only in the extraordinary phenomenon of 'seeing' her through my ears. I'll bet she enjoys her bit of fun.'

'Philip, please!'

'Oh, lord. I always forget how prudish you are! After six years of married life you really should be a bit more sophisticated. I know you think I'm coarse — what you won't remember is that I live in a hospital where we

14

call a spade a spade. I simply can't acquire your romantic attitude towards such things.'

'It . . . it isn't that, Philip. I just don't think it's fair to Sister Whatshername — Bristow — to talk about her like that.'

'Oh, gossip, you mean. Won't do her any harm. If she is as I think, every doctor and student in the place will know it.'

'I still don't think it's fair to talk about her like that.'

She broke off, surprised at her own vehemence. What did it really matter what men thought about Sister Bristow! Or was this some inner defence mechanism at work? If Philip who was usually so insensitive, could hear things in the nurse's voice, perhaps he'd hear 'things' in her voice, too!

But Philip was listening to himself, enjoying, as he always did, the sound of his own rhetoric.

'It's just come back to mind that I heard something about that woman not so long ago. Someone said she was having an affair with one of our chaps . . . now, let me see . . . yes, I remember, Bill Aden. Might not be true, of course, but it's more than likely. They're both unmarried. He's not a bad looking fellow, either — might easily catch a woman's eye if she was on the look out for a randy man!'

'Philip!' She simply could not control the

horror in her voice. For one terrible moment, she wondered if he were saying all this on purpose; he could have found out somehow about Bill and her. If he had done so, this was about the most perfectly sadistic method of torture he could have thought up. But when he spoke again, his voice was mild, even a trifle apologetic.

'Sorry, darling. Forgot you didn't care for juicy tit-bits. Though for the life of me, I can't see that it matters. There are always masses of intrigues going on in a hospital — one might just as well face facts. Men and women are thrown together and the women are usually as frustrated as hell. Can't blame them for setting their caps at the doctors, especially a psychiatrist like Aden. They probably think he knows all the right ways to treat them in bed, understanding their needs, that kind of thing.'

He waited for her to comment but it was several seconds before she could trust herself to speak.

Philip must be wrong, not Bill, not Bill . . . he'd have told me. 'The truth, the whole truth, and nothing but the truth, my love — that's the way it's going to be between us. I hate half-truths even more, I think, than a downright lie. Trust between lovers is essential. If you don't love me, I'd*

16

rather know it. I couldn't bear for you to pretend . . .'

'Couldn't we change the subject?' she asked. Her voice sounded extraordinarily calm and a little bored.

'Sorry!' He took her hand again and patted it as if she were a small child. 'Can't seem to help my mind running on sex. You'd have thought that belting I took would have had the opposite effect. I suppose they've been bunging me full of drugs and shoved in one with a side-kick.' He laughed at his own joke. 'Must ask Matron what she's been giving me. Might even be Sister Bristow. Maybe she gave me something on purpose hoping to seduce me while you were away.'

I simply can't stand any more of this . . . Philip at his worst.

He pulled her arm, dragging her down on top of him and began to kiss her. She struggled to free herself but not before she felt his lips, hot and wet and hungry on her mouth. It was all she could do not to wipe furiously with her free hand.

'What's wrong, Noni?'

'Someone might come in, Philip!'

'So what? I'm your husband, aren't I?'

'But they wouldn't be keeping you here in hospital if they thought it was all right for you to lead a . . . a normal life.'

'Good God, Noni, I only want to *kiss* you!'

But even that is more than I can stand. It's too soon . . . too soon after Bill.

She was saved by a young nurse arriving with Philip's tea-tray.

The girl seemed to recognize her.

'Oh, Mrs Brisbane, I didn't know you were here. I'll fetch another cup.'

'No, no, don't do that. I have to get home. I was just going.' *Calm down, for God's sake.* 'Philip, you don't mind, do you, darling? I didn't get back from Eileen's till lunchtime and I haven't even unpacked yet.'

Philip sighed. His voice was suddenly petulant.

'Oh, well, if you have to go, I suppose I must grin and bear it.' The nurse put the tray on his lap and gently lifted his hands onto it.

'There's your tea, Mr Brisbane — the plate this side has paste sandwiches — the other side is cake. It's Dundee and not stale!'

Noni watched his long, beautiful hands fumble clumsily with the crockery. Philip the surgeon, whose hands had been rock-steady working with miracle precision, reduced to trembling uncertainty. The picture appalled her.

'I don't really *have* to go — the packing can wait till later. I'll stay and have tea with you, darling.'

18

The young nurse looked pleased.

'Oh, then you can help Mr Brisbane if he needs anything. I'll bring another cup.'

'Nice little thing — what's she look like?' Philip asked, picking up a sandwich.

'She's dark-skinned — Jamaican, I should think. Pretty!'

Philip sighed.

'You're going to have to be my eyes in future, Noni. I dare say it will be a bore for you having to describe everyone and everything. You won't change anything at home, will you? The furniture, for instance . . . I want it all left just as it was before . . . before my accident. I can remember where most things are . . . spent quite a bit of time lying here thinking about it. Tell Mrs Reeves and the daily, too, that everything's got to be kept in exactly the same place.'

'Yes, Philip, of course I will!'

He took another bite of the sandwich.

'I'm afraid the last time you were here, I was behaving rather badly. I know I did nothing but complain about my career going for six and wishing to hell I'd been killed like that other poor devil. I was so sorry for myself, I'd forgotten to be sorry for you. Won't be much fun for you, Noni, tied to a blind man. Then there's the financial side. Of course, we'll get heavy damages — there's no doubt whose fault it was and the other insurance firm has already agreed to pay in full. All the same, we're going to have to cut down, I should think; alter our way of life quite a bit.'

How can I say that none of it matters because I won't be staying for long? I can't . . . I can't . . . Bill you must understand. I — I can be truthful with you but not with Philip.

The nurse returned with another cup of tea. Noni drank it gratefully. She felt utterly exhausted. It wasn't just three successive nights without sleep; the nervous tension of the last hour more than anything had emptied her of any vestige of energy.

Somewhere in the hospital, Bill is working. Tuesday is one of his days here. A quarter to four. Will he have finished for the day? If I leave now, I could go and see him. No, better not. He's promised to phone me at home tonight anyway. Can I wait until then for him to tell me there's nothing between him and Sister Bristow? I'll believe him if he denies it. I don't think it's true. I just need to hear him say it isn't . . .

'She's right about the cake — not bad at all!'

Philip sounded happier. Maybe she could go now.

'What . . . what will you do from now until you go to sleep?' she asked, lifting the tray off the bed.

He looked suddenly tired and lay back against the pillows.

'Oh, lie here — listen to the radio, I expect. One or two of the doctors will probably look in. Then, of course, there's the usual grim nightly battle of bed-making, washing, temperatures, bedpans and doctor's round. I never realized what my wretched patients had to put up with until I landed up here.'

'Doctors always make bad patients, I've heard. It won't be for much longer, Philip.'

'No, thank God. Look, Noni, if you're going home now, there are one or two things I'd like you to do — phone calls, mostly. I've made a list here — perhaps you'd see to it. There's another list of things I want you to bring tomorrow. Okay?'

His lists were barely legible, the lines running down the page and sometimes over-lapping. For the third time since she had come into the room, she was shaken with pity.

'You can read them? The nurse who brought my lunch said they were quite clear.'

'Yes, of course. You've managed very well!'

He grinned.

'You sound like a blasted school mistress.'

21

She drove home in the Mini, her movements entirely automatic. The road out of Hadingbourne was one she had travelled so often, she knew every turn and cross-road. After two miles, the street-lighting ended abruptly and she was in the country, only half a mile now from West Martials, the pretty little Georgian house she'd always loved so much and been so terribly unhappy in!

She turned into the drive and garaged the car. There was a large dark space beside her now — where Philip's Jag had been and would never be again. It was being repaired, of course, but it would have to be sold. Blind men can't drive . . .

Slowly she walked up the flagged path towards the lights and warmth and Mrs Reeves' welcome. Home! Yet still the loneliest place in the world because there was no Bill waiting with open arms to receive her.

It was nine o'clock before he phoned. She felt sick with relief at hearing his voice. He sounded rather irritable.

'I've been trying for over an hour to get you!'

'I'm so sorry, darling. Father phoned after supper asking about Philip; then Eileen rang up to ask if I'd had any trouble; and a girl friend phoned. I tried to cut them short but you know what it is.'

Don't be cross, Bill. I've had about as much as I can stand . . .

'How are you, darling? Everything all right? I've been worried about you!'

'Oh, Bill!' She paused, fighting against the hot stinging tears that had filled her eyes.

'Darling? You all right?'

'Yes . . . Bill, I love you!'

'And I love you — it's hell. I'm missing you so much I'm finding it hard to be sensible. Do you know, I very nearly stopped by your house on my way back to the flat?'

'What time?'

'Five-thirty. Would you have been there?'

'No! I . . . I had to stay a bit until Philip had had tea. Bill, it was awful — *awful!*'

'Oh, God!' There was a pause. In the background, a very faint conversation was taking place — the line was not too good. 'Were you cross-questioned?'

'No, not much. It wasn't that . . . I . . . I just felt so — so sorry for him.'

'Yes, of course. But that's inevitable, isn't it?'

'Somehow it was worse than ever.'

'But you're still going to leave him?' He sounded anxious.

'Yes! No! Bill, I'm not sure now if I'll be *able* to!' Her voice was rising. She was becoming a little hysterical.

'Look, darling, don't let's talk about that right now. You're tired — and I am, too, and your nerves are on edge. We can talk about it all next time we're together, calmly and sensibly. There's no hurry.'

She felt suddenly calmer. She remembered Sister Bristow. She said:

'Bill, Philip said he's heard some gossip about a nurse at the hospital called Sister Bristow — that she'd been having an affair.'

She waited for his reply but the line seemed dead.

'Bill?'

'Yes! What about Sister Bristow?'

'Well, Philip said he'd heard a rumour it was with you!'

Now he'll laugh — I love to hear his laugh. Bill, why aren't you saying anything.

'That's all in the past, Noni — water under the bridge!'

She was staggered.

'You mean . . . it's *true*?'

'*Was* true. Not now — not since I've known you. That's the truth, Noni.'

She believed him — so why was she so hurt? So shocked?

'Noni, darling, listen to me. It's all over — *finished*!'

'But you never told me about her!'

I sound like an accusing wife!

24

'Why in God's name should I? There was nothing important to tell you. I wasn't in love with her — or she with me. It was just a — a mutual convenience.'

Am I a mutual convenience? No, don't say that —

'Noni, I'm going to drive over to see you. I can be over in half an hour.'

'No, Bill, not here. We agreed that we'd never meet here.'

'Then somewhere else. I've *got* to see you.'

Temptation swept over her and a terrible weak longing to say yes, yes, yes. But if she gave way this time, she'd give way the next and the next and the next. She'd got to learn to go on living without him — for a while longer anyway. They'd talked it all out. Whenever it was possible, they'd be together, a night, two nights — for as long as possible. But the hitherto daily meetings in the hospital, in cafés and pubs and in their cars had got to stop. It was far too dangerous. They were both very well known in the district and could easily be recognized. People might start talking and then it would be impossible to keep the truth from Philip. Bill might not care, but she did. She couldn't give Philip another shock so soon after his terrible accident. Bill had agreed.

'Noni, why don't you answer me? Darling,

say something, please. Are you crying, Noni? . . . '

'I'm all right, Bill — really. I . . . I can't meet you. I daren't. I think if I saw you tonight, I'd never have the strength to come home again. I love you too much now — it weakens me.'

'You're not going to worry all night — about the Bristow woman?'

'No, I'd almost forgotten her. I'm glad you didn't love her.'

'Forget her. There's no one in my life but you, Noni. There never will be anyone else. I don't know how I got through today without you. I've missed you desperately. Believe it or not, I've been wanting to make love to you, too. I thought this morning I'd be immune to that particular temptation for at least the next week. Is it the same for you?'

'No. I just want to be with you.'

There was no physical desire left in her. She was too tired, too deeply depressed and Bill was too far away. If she could be with him, it would be to feel his arms holding her and to know he was there. Sex was unimportant.

His voice came low and husky across the distance between them. He sounded near to her, in the room with her.

26

'I don't think I could be with you without wanting you, Noni.'

And suddenly she did want him. Her need was as physical as his — born of his. But not for the sweet pleasure of sensation — for something else — for the oblivion, the complete negation of self that followed their love-making. Lying satiated in his arms, there were no more problems; no frustrations; there was no loneliness. She was what God had intended her to be, all woman, warm, alive, fulfilled. Oh, to feel like that now!

'Bill, Bill! I'm missing you so much!'

'I know, sweetheart. It's hell. Let me come to you.'

'No, no, not here!'

'Then somewhere else?'

'Not tonight!' How could she explain? Did he realize how terrified she was that selfishness was going to end up over-ruling even pity? They had had three nights together — three whole days and nights. That should be enough . . . but it wasn't . . . not for either of them. It merely gave them an appetite for more.

'Noni, darling, are you there? Say something to me. I'm so worried about you. I know you must have had a lousy day — far worse than mine. I wish . . . I wish to hell you'd get it over with and let me take you away. It would be better for Philip, too, you know.'

'Oh, darling don't. We've been through all this. It's too late . . . we should have gone off before the accident . . . '

'Noni, you aren't going to back down on that promise you gave me? You're coming away with me eventually, when Philip is on his feet?'

He sounded frantic. Did he really believe she had the power to put him out of her life completely? Didn't he realize that she loved him? *Loved* him! Without him she had been only half alive. Knowing him, being loved by him, had transformed not only her but the whole of her life. She'd *known* marriage with Philip was a mistake but without understanding why it was all so unsatisfactory, disappointing. It wasn't just the sex side of it. Philip as a person, a companion, a friend, a lover — each facet had always been inadequate for her needs.

'Bill, I love you! But I've just got to have time — call it time to square my conscience if you like.' She sounded suddenly aggrieved. 'I *thought* you understood!'

'Noni, darling, I do. I'm not trying to rush you for my own sake. It's for yours — and Philip's. I know you find that hard to believe, but it's true. He has to find out in the end

28

and he's going to be pretty bitter about these months of pretence.'

'More bitter than if his wife walked out on him when he was as far down as a man could be?'

'Sometimes it is easier to take all the knocks at once. There is a limit, you know, to how wretched a human being can feel. Once you've hit bottom, it is inevitable that everything begins to improve. You're going to feed Philip a lot of false hopes and then dash them in his face.'

'Bill, don't!'

'All right, we'll talk about something else. Noni, promise me you won't lie awake thinking about Sarah Bristow. You won't, will you? I'm not saying the friendship was platonic but neither of us ever pretended it was anything but sex.'

'And that means nothing?'

'Not without love, Noni. It's just like having a drink or a meal when you're hungry.'

'And was it that way for her, too?'

'Yes, of course!'

But how could it be — for a woman? For a man, maybe, but surely a women had to be at least a little bit emotionally involved. Maybe this Sarah Bristow had loved Bill and he didn't know it.

'Noni, what are you wearing?'

She smiled.

'A negligée. I had a bath and changed when I got back from the hospital.'

'The pink one?'

'No, darling! I'll only ever wear that for you. It's an old blue dressing-gown, really. I just said 'negligée' to make it sound more glamorous!'

'Silly girl — you'd look glamorous in anything. Or nothing. To me.'

'You said last night I wasn't beautiful!'

'You're not. You've got a funny little face. Your nose is too long and your mouth is too big. It's lucky I like long noses and big mouths.'

She felt happy. Only Bill could do this to her — make her smile when a moment before she had been close to tears. She remembered last night's conversation so well. 'Let's play the truth game, Bill. Tell me truly if you think I'm beautiful!' And later, Bill had said: 'I'm much better looking for a man than you are for a woman. Everyone will say: How can such a handsome man have married such a plain woman — until they look at your figure — then they'll understand! Of course, your eyes aren't bad — I might even be forced to admit that they are beautiful. Beautiful, laughing eyes . . . '

'Are you smiling, Noni?'

'Uh-huh!'

'I'm never going to be able to sleep tonight. I shall lie awake all night wanting you — wishing I had you snuggled up beside me. What are you wearing under the dressing-gown-cum-negligée?'

'Bra — pants . . . that's all.'

'Wish I could take them off.'

'Bill, this phone call will be costing you a fortune. We've been on for hours.'

'So what? It's my money I'm spending.'

She hesitated and the silence dragged on a little too long. Bill spoke, his voice sounding withdrawn, hurt.

'Are you expecting a call from Philip? Do you want me to ring off?'

'Oh, Bill, no!'

How had he guessed? Philip had said 'I'll ring you about nine, Noni, to hear if everything is okay at home.' If the line was engaged too long, he might wonder . . .

'Don't ever lie to me, Noni. I'm not cross — I understand. After all, it *is* Philip's phone.'

'Bill, please . . . ' she began, but he was saying goodbye. Even his '*I love you, Noni,*' before he rang off could not make things better. He was hurt and she had hurt him.

The phone rang again almost at once. Its shrill ringing made her jump. The hand she put out to lift the receiver trembled.

31

'Noni? Who in heaven's name have you been talking to? Susan, I suppose — the way you two girls gossip is past all belief. One of these days I'm going to make you pay the phone bill out of your allowance.'

'I'm sorry, Philip. Have you been trying to get me for long?'

'For at least half an hour. I'm supposed to have had my light out twenty minutes ago — it's gone ten.'

'Philip, I'm *sorry*. I'd no idea it was so late.'

How long had she and Bill been talking?

'Well, how's everything? Did you find those letters from my accountant?'

He continued to question her for another five minutes. She did her best to satisfy him. Already that potent combination of guilt and pity were dictating her responses to him. A month ago, she would have told him to cope with his own affairs and not trouble her with them when she was tired. But then, a month ago Philip wouldn't have had to ask for her help; nor would she have been so tired.

'Well, better get some shut-eye. You'll be in in the morning then, Noni?'

'Yes, of course. About eleven?'

'Can't you make it before then?' He sounded petulant.

'Yes — I'll try and be there by ten.'

She'd have to alter that hair appointment

. . . maybe in the afternoon.

She replaced the receiver and turned out the sitting room lights. In the glow from the fire, the room looked softer, kindlier. She stood for a moment in the doorway, staring at it as if she was seeing it all for the first — or last — time.

She had taken such care planning the mood of this room, wanting it to have both elegance and comfort. The carpets were an impractical pale yellow, the curtains silver blue. The warm red-brown of the mahogany furniture shone softly against the background of silver blue wallpaper. A yellow brocade Knole sofa lay in a pool of light beneath the red silk shaded lamps.

She turned and went upstairs. Fatigue overcame her. Hardly able to see from eyes that were sticky and hot with want of sleep, she removed her make-up, brushed her hair, cleaned her teeth and fell into bed.

The phone rang. She wasn't sure if she had been sleeping for a minute or an hour. In the darkness, her arm reached out for the receiver and she laid it on the pillow by her head. Dazedly, she wondered what accident Philip was being called out to this time.

'Noni? It's Bill!'

She woke up. Fully.

'Noni?'

'Yes, darling?'

'Did I wake you? You sound so sleepy. *Did* I wake you?'

'Yes, but I'm glad.'

She cradled the receiver on the pillow. It lay there like Bill's head against her cheek.

'I couldn't go to bed without saying I'm sorry and that I love you desperately. I was pretty nasty a while ago — about you waiting for Philip's call, I mean. Am I forgiven?'

'Yes, of *course*!'

'I'm a fool!' Bill said. He sounded quite cheerful about it. 'You'll just have to bear with me, Noni. I suppose it sounds crazy to you but I'm childishly jealous.'

'Jealous? Of *Philip*?'

'Yes! His disabilities give him first call on you — I resent it even while logic tells me that I've no right to do so.'

'Darling, don't. You come first in my heart — now and always. I love you. I've loved you since that first evening . . . '

'The dance!'

'Yes, darling. The hospital dance. You came up behind me and said: 'May I?' and I was too surprised to say 'no, thank you'.'

Bill laughed, remembering.

'You looked surprised, too, but no more than I was. You see, I was just leaving. I found it all pretty boring and then Sarah said: 'Bet

34

you don't ask Mrs Brisbane for a dance'.'

Now she was laughing too.

'I still don't understand why you had to be 'dared' to do it.'

'I've told you a dozen times, my love. Your husband was a very senior surgeon and had a reputation for being — well, standoffish. He'd snub his subordinates far more often than he would look at them.'

Noni tried to see Philip once more through the eyes of the hospital staff. He could be pompous and curt. His own faultless efficiency made him very intolerant of mistakes. But to be actually frightened of him . . .

'I'd only been asked for duty dances up to then. It was a lovely dance, Bill.'

'I fell in love with you that very second I put my arms round you. Remember the tune, Noni? 'Lady in Red'. You've still got the record I gave you, haven't you?'

'Yes!'

'I've got mine, too. Hang on a moment, darling, and I'll put it on . . . ' He rushed off before she could say anything. She smiled into the darkness. He could be so young — so impulsive, so very very sweet . . .

'There, can you hear it, darling?'

She listened, her eyes closed. She was back on the dance floor, in Bill's arms. She was trembling. Bill was holding her far too close. His cheek was against hers. She whispered: 'Someone will see us!' He laughed and whispered back: 'I hope it gives them the same kick it's giving me!'

'Have you gone to sleep, Noni?'

'No!'

'Let me come and make love to you!'

'No!'

'No, no, a thousand times no! All right, my darling, you go off to sleep but I'm ordering you to dream of me. Do you understand?'

'Yes!'

'At last an affirmative!'

'Love me?'

'Yes!'

'A lot or a little?'

'Yes!' Their laughter mingled over the wires.

'Good night, darling. I love you.'

'I love you, too, Bill.'

After that, she could not sleep.

2

The two nurses were off duty. Sister Bristow was lying on her back on her bed, smoking a cigarette. Her room-mate, Nancy Coutts, sat at the dressing table curling her blonde hair. They had both put in a long eight-hour stretch, Sarah in the Maternity Wing, Nancy in the Children's Ward.

'Mrs Parker lost her baby!' Sarah said as they continued their discussion of the day's events. She was a heavily built girl — red-haired, dark-eyed which gave her an unusual gipsy look. She was extremely attractive to the opposite sex, but was not, despite the fact that she was only a year off thirty, either married or engaged to be married. Nancy, her slighter, more feminine colleague, was to be married next year to young Dr Mathews. Nancy thought it strange that Sarah was still single but then the facets of Sarah's character she most admired, self-reliance, determination, authoritativeness, were the very ones which scared off the young men who were initially physically attracted to her. She was too aggressive for them; too domineering, too male. They were frightened of her as well as attracted by her.

'I thought she was having a Caesarian?'

Sarah nodded.

'Mr Phelps did it. Of course, I wouldn't breathe this to another soul, but, Janet (she named the theatre sister), told me he bungled the job. If Mr Brisbane had done it, the baby would have survived.'

'Will there be trouble with a capital T?'

Sarah blew out a cloud of smoke, frowning.

'No! It was one of those tricky moments with the outcome debatable — mother or child, you know. But Janet says Mr Brisbane would have taken the chance and saved both. But you can't prove a thing like that. For heaven's sake, Nancy, don't let on I told you.'

'You know you can trust me!'

Nancy was one of the few close friends she had made since she'd come to Hadingbourne Hospital — girl friends, that is. There'd been plenty of boy friends. She frowned now, the thick dark eyebrows forming a heavy frame to her almond-shaped eyes. For a while she'd believed Bill Aden was getting really serious. She'd even started to daydream of the possible future — Bill, who was the most eligible and by far the best-looking doctor on the staff, coming to the conclusion that his bachelor days were over.

Fool! she thought bitterly. For Bill it had never been more than a friendly convenience between equals, friends. She'd been an idiot to imagine anything else in their brief affair. He had someone else now, she was certain of it, though for a moment she wasn't too sure who. She wondered if he was back from sick leave; wondered if he'd really been 'sick' or if he'd been off on a spree.

'It's terrible about Mr Brisbane, isn't it?'

Nancy's voice, distorted by the hairpin now clenched between her teeth, broke in on Sarah's thoughts.

'Hell for him. I saw him yesterday. You know, Nancy, you've got to admire his guts. He was actually flirting with me. You'd have expected him to be far too depressed to think of anything but that ghastly accident.'

Nancy giggled.

'Fancy Mr Brisbane flirting — doesn't seem like him a bit, does it? I mean, everyone says he's so bad tempered.'

'Don't you believe it — at least, only with the doctors — not with the nurses. He's always been perfectly polite and reasonable with me. Personally I don't think he deserves the reputation he's got in this hospital. It's inefficiency that gets his goat and I can't say I blame him. It drives me round the bend when one of those silly little student nurses forgets something basic like a bed pan or breaks her third thermometer in one day.'

'That's because you're so efficient yourself, Sarah. I wouldn't wonder if you got to be matron one day, really I wouldn't.'

But I don't want to be matron of any hospital! Sarah thought, suddenly deeply depressed by her friend's praise. She wanted to get married, have a home, children, perhaps. She wanted to give up the hard slogging work in a hospital and take it easy, let some man provide for her, with all the luxuries she craved and had never been able to afford. One wasn't likely to acquire them on a nurse's pay, nor even on a Matron's.

'I passed Mrs Brisbane in the corridor — she must have been visiting him. She looked ever so pale and ill. Been a shock for her, too. I wonder what they'll do now. I mean, he'll never be able to work again, will he?'

'No! A brilliant career cut off in its prime. Still, I hear he's getting full compensation from the insurance company. Mary heard Mr Harvey telling the house surgeon. He'll just retire early, that's all, on full pension.'

Nancy put the last curler in and sat back, easing her aching shoulders.

'All the same, money can't really compensate, can it?'

'No, but it can make life a damn sight easier!' Sarah said succinctly.

Nancy began to discuss in detail the poverty stricken years ahead of her and her young doctor fiancé. Sarah stopped listening for she had heard most of it before. Her mind swung away to a different problem — that of young Susan Mason on Men's Surgical. The silly little fool had got herself pregnant with one of the young medical students and Sarah had caught her late one night crying in the Dispensary. Then the story had come out. Sarah felt sorry for the girl who was a first-year student and had the kind of parents whom she couldn't possibly talk to. She'd refused to help her, of course, telling her she was probably mistaken anyway and to wait another month before she tried to do anything desperate. Ever since then, the girl had clung like a limpet to Sarah and now another month was up and there was no longer any doubt that the girl was pregnant.

'Help me, Sister Bristow, please, *please*! I'll kill myself if you don't help me.'

There'd been a time in Sarah's life when she, too, had needed help. She'd been about the same age but she'd been luckier — her father was a doctor and he'd arranged an abortion at a reputable private clinic. She promised to think the matter over. She was tempted to help her because she could not divorce Susan's plight from her own past, but Susan was already over the date when a legal abortion was possible.

Not for the first time, Sarah considered how hard was the life of a nurse — long hours, bad pay and practically no privacy. A secretary or a clerk or a factory worker was better off in all these ways. In work of that sort, a girl could take time off, have a baby, get it adopted and no one any the wiser. But just let young Susan Mason try to talk Matron into letting her have a six month's vacation to visit relatives in New Zealand!

She sighed deeply. What with one thing and another, she was getting fed up with hospital life. The fun of those early years was beginning to tarnish. *She* was beginning to tarnish. At close on thirty, she looked at times thirty-five, even forty after night duty. Oh, she was still attractive to men, but somehow none of them ever seemed to want more than an affair. Marriage wasn't part of their plan when they 'fell in love'.

She looked enviously at Nancy — silly, empty-headed, frivolous, flirtatious — yet this was Nancy's third proposal and, so it would seem, her last. Nancy was the type men liked because she was helpless, appealing, admiring. The brainier the man, the sillier the woman he chose. It was strange, really. One would have supposed intelligence to require a matching intelligence. Men were scared because she, Sarah, had a good brain, a quick critical mind and, so Bill Aden had once informed her, a way of making them feel inferior.

A wry smile touched her lips. Except perhaps for Bill, most of the men she had slept with were inferior. But it wasn't her fault if they were fools. There were so few men about — in the hospital anyway — whom she felt she could really respect. Poor Mr Brisbane was one of them. He was a brilliant surgeon with a cool, precise brain that never wavered in emergencies. Attractive, too, with a strong, rather sensuous face and green eyes which could strike like lightning on any kind of failure around him. It still shocked her after all these weeks to think that his career was at an end. No wonder his wife looked the way Nancy decribed. Sarah wondered if she was the kind of woman who could face disasters of such magnitude or if she would go weepy and uncontrollable and be fool enough to pity her husband.

'You know, Nancy, if I'd been blinded like Mr Brisbane, I think the hardest part of all to bear would be other people's pity.'

Nancy's eyebrows shot up in surprise.

'Would it, Sarah? I think I'd rather enjoy having everyone make a fuss of me. I mean, it would be some compensation to know that everyone else understood what one was going through.'

'Well, I think it would be hell. I'll bet you anything Mr Brisbane isn't the kind of man to want everyone feeling sorry for him. I'm going to find some way of going to see him tomorrow. He interests me. I just can't understand how he can be so cheerful at a time like this. Is it just bravado or is he really a very brave man? I want to know.'

Nancy giggled suggestively.

'You've always rather fancied him, haven't you, Sarah? If he hadn't been married, would you have set your cap at him?'

Sarah turned her face away to hide her annoyance. Despite her cotton-wool brain, Nancy could sometimes hit the target without knowing how she got there. Sarah was absolutely sure that not another soul in the hospital knew of her secret attraction to Philip Brisbane. One of the things which had most attracted her was that he totally ignored her. As a rule, men didn't ignore her when she chose to interest them. Philip Brisbane had been immune — or at least, until yesterday. Then, for the first time, he

44

had really noticed her.

'You must be Sister Bristow — the girl with the husky voice!'

She had been too surprised to answer. He'd gone on:

'It is you, isn't it, Sister? The one with the red hair?'

She had felt flattered — the more so because of his reputation for being remote and distant with all the nurses. It was generally accepted that he was completely devoted to his wife and not one of 'those' — 'those' being the married men who were always hoping for a little fun on the side.

Nancy disappeared to have a bath and Sarah was left alone. She was tired and a little depressed. There was no man in her life at the moment and she had the feeling that she was at the crossroads. She'd been nursing for eleven years now — it was too long. The next few years must decide whether she was to marry or not. Marriage had suddenly assumed a vast importance. Perhaps it was Nancy getting engaged. Perhaps it was just that she was fed up with hospital life and needed a holiday.

'What I need this minute is a drink!' she told herself ruefully, and helped herself from the gin she kept in her cupboard. As the spirits touched her dry throat, she thought how much more she would be enjoying it if she were out with a man who would later take her to bed. Sarah needed sex. There was little romance attached to these purely physical requirements. Her approach to sex was more akin to that of a man. There were occasions when she felt that something was lacking and knew that it must be love. She had wanted more from him that Bill Aden had been prepared to give her. It had hit her harder than she thought when Bill, in the most tactful way possible, put an end to the affair. But she was too honest a person to kid herself that she had been in love with him. She had only been in love once and that was with the middle-aged pathologist who singled her out from the other young virgin students and taught her everything he said she ought to know. That love had turned to bitter hate when she discovered he was already married and had no intention of leaving his wife. Since then there'd been many men who had taken her to bed but none whom she had loved. She wondered sometimes if she ever would fall in love again. She knew that she would marry without love if the chance came her way but she was still just young enough to hope that it would.

On a sudden impulse, she put down her drink and went over to the dressing table. There she sat down and following Nancy's example, she began the task of putting curlers in her hair.

3

Bill was tired. He hadn't slept well and this morning there'd been a full list of patients, one following the other into his room in a long endless stream. To each person, he had to give something of himself. As a psychiatrist there was no easy remedy to dish out for the disturbed mind the way a G.P. could dish out pills. He had to get into his patients' minds, feel their difficulties and perplexities. Today it seemed as if a little of every patient's problem had been transferred to him.

There would be no one else to see until two o'clock. He should be at lunch but he had stayed behind in his room to think.

'Fine one I am to try to deal with other people's mental disturbances!' he thought, a momentary smile crossing his face. 'I'm more than a little mentally disturbed myself!'

Noni was *his* problem. Noni whom he loved as he had never imagined it possible to love a woman. Yet it looked as if, now that he had finally found her, it was simply to lose her again. He didn't doubt that she loved him. But Noni was feminine from the top of her head to the tip of her toes. She would balance one man's need against another's — and Philip would win.

His main trouble was that he no longer knew if he had the moral right to try to take her away from Brisbane. There was little doubt that he could make her happier than Brisbane could ever do or had ever done. But the fact was, she was Brisbane's wife and the man was blind. Maybe if she stayed with him, sacrificing her own happiness, she would succeed in building up some kind of life for him, for them both. But *could* she? There was no love to help and guide her — only pity and as he, Bill, had told her over and over again, a man like Brisbane would loathe pity. It would degrade him, demoralize him.

But, argued the little voice of truth within Bill's mind, would Brisbane necessarily recognize the fact that Noni was only staying with him because she was so sorry for him? He didn't know she'd been about to leave him. Unless Noni or Bill were to tell him, he'd never know. Therefore he might take as his natural right the help and support she gave him.

'*I'd* know all right!'

His thought was so strong, he actually spoke the words aloud.

'*But then I love her! Brisbane doesn't. I know what she is feeling from every tiny* expression on her face; from every nuance of her voice!'

'How do you know Brisbane doesn't love her?'

'Because she has told me so.'

'But that may not be the truth. She may only think this because she has fallen in love with you and wants to think it. His kind of love may be different from yours. You can't be sure.'

'No, damn it, I can't!' Bill told himself wretchedly.

He was desperately tempted to go along to Brisbane's room and have it all out with him. He'd imagined the conversation a thousand times.

'I'm in love with your wife; I want you to divorce her!'

There would be surprise at first.

'You — and Noni! I never knew!'

'We're both sorry. We didn't mean it to happen. I felt I must tell you the truth. Will you let her go?'

'Well, as a matter of fact, we haven't been getting along too well. I won't stand in Noni's way if she's sure this is what she wants.'

'She's sure!'

Bill knew that this kind of imaginary conversation was laced with the unreality of television scripts and cheap literature. As if any real-life dialogue could follow that pattern! Brisbane would fight for Noni and Bill would be the last to blame him.

If he only knew whether Brisbane really loved her! There lay the crux of the matter. If he knew that was so, he'd get a transfer to another hospital and never see Noni again. The very last thing he would have been able to do was to take away the adored wife of a severely handicapped man. Was Noni wrong about her husband? It was difficult to be sure for she was intensely loyal and except for the brief unhappy account of her married life the first time they'd been away together, she'd never spoken an intentionally derogatory word about him. He had assumed the facts from Noni's behaviour. She was so clearly starved of tenderness and not only grateful but innocently surprised when he made some thoughtful little gesture prompted by his love for her. Why else should she have been surprised unless she had never had the chance to take such little things for granted. For example, he loved to go on kissing her after their love-making was over.

'It's so lovely to be loved *afterwards*!' she had said. 'But don't you feel sleepy, darling?'

What else could he assume but that her husband took what he wanted and fell asleep as soon as he had had it, regardless of Noni's needs. He knew Brisbane's type — not so much selfish as utterly insensitive. She would never have married him if she had been older, with more experience of life. She'd told him in detail about the sheltered childhood her father, the Brigadier, had insisted upon. No army school or private school for Noni. It was a governess until she was thirteen and then a convent with old-fashioned strict ideas on shielding young ladies from the facts of life. No wonder that at eighteen she had been flattered by the proposal of the up and coming young surgeon, ten years her senior. Her father had approved the match despite Brisbane's rather humble origins because already Brisbane was being spoken of as a top surgeon and was obviously destined for the top of his profession.

Well, Brisbane had made the grade all right — all the way up to the top with frightening speed. One thing Bill would never underestimate was Brisbane's quality as a surgeon. 'Brilliant' was a fair enough description. Now he was blind . . .

What would the man do with his life now? Bill asked himself. What *could* he do? Lecture, perhaps, to students? Or would he be happier in some entirely new field? Reflexology? That would seem to be a terrible come-down after surgery. Could a man like Brisbane be content to do nothing? According to the rumours Bill had heard, there would be the fullest compensation so Brisbane would not really need to work. Somehow one couldn't imagine Brisbane leading a life of leisure.

The problem of Brisbane's future had become suddenly and fantastically his own. Deep down Bill knew he was fighting, just as Noni's husband must be fighting, not to accept the truth; because the truth meant blindness for Brisbane and he could not have Noni at the price of a blind man's happiness. Even if he were willing to disregard Brisbane's feelings, Noni was not. Deep down he knew it, but he couldn't accept it — not yet.

The door opened and Noni stood there. For a moment he wasn't sure if she was real, so unexpected was her visit and at a time when his mind was so full of her.

'Bill! I was so afraid you'd be at lunch.'

He jumped to his feet and went round his desk, pushing the door closed behind her. He took her in his arms.

She clung to him fiercely, her face hidden from him against his shoulder.

'Noni, Noni!'

He held her strained against him, not with

passion so much as with the need to imprison her within the circle of his arms; keep her with him. Only like this could he be sure she loved him, needed him as much as he needed her.

'Bill!'

She pulled a little away from him and touched his face with her fingers tenderly, her eyes searching his. Gradually the strained lines of her mouth eased and with a half-smile she whispered:

'I do love you so much!'

He felt his own love for her choking him so that he could not speak. He bent his head and kissed her fiercely.

For an instant, he felt her mouth responding, returning his kisses. Then she drew away, her voice trembling.

'Someone might come in, Bill!'

'Oh, hell!' He let her go and sat down on the edge of his desk as she seated herself in his chair. He thought she looked very beautiful. She was wearing a simple suit of some kind of nobbly material, the collar edged in black and making a dark contrast to the ash blonde hair framing her face. The grey-blue shirt exactly matched her eyes. She might have stepped off the cover of one of the glossy magazines, he thought. But the doctor in him noted the tiny lines of tension round those eyes and the pretty soft mouth he so loved to kiss and kiss. Her hands were restless as the slim fingers played with the catch of her handbag.

'Bill, I've been with Philip all morning.' Her voice was uneven, betraying to his observant mind, the strain which she was under.

'How is he?'

'In marvellous spirits, Bill. This is what I came to tell you — Philip has seen Herod, you know, the Ophthalmic Surgeon. It seems he has more residual vision than Herod had at first hoped for. An operation might be possible — to improve the sight of one eye.'

Bill drew in his breath sharply.

'You mean, *he may not be blind after all*?'

'Philip seems to think not. He says if he can get back full sight of one eye, he could go on with his work — he's sure of it. Bill, I'm so worried. Can it be true? Harvey told me it was quite out of the question after the accident. Could he have been wrong? Oh, I wish I understood more about all this.'

Her uneasiness was communicated to him and the first swift rush of pleasure in her news began to fade.

'It does seem a bit odd,' he said. 'Yet I can't believe Herod would have raised Philip's hopes like that without good reason. It would be so appalling if he had to face being blind all over again. He's quite certain about it?'

'Philip is, yes! He's full of plans and hopes and wouldn't even let me question him on the facts. 'Take my word for it, Noni,' he said. 'If Herod operates, I'll be able to see again. There isn't a man to touch him here or in America or anywhere else in the world'.'

Bill was silent. He had no inside knowledge of Philip's case and knew nothing about diseases or conditions of eyes except in their relation to mental disturbances. But if it were true, then . . .

'Noni, darling, do you realize what this news means . . . to us, to you and me?'

She looked at him now with eyes that were shining, unashamedly naked in their expression of love.

'Do you imagine that I've not thought about it? Last night I was so afraid. I thought we were going to lose each other. I couldn't see any way out for us. Now, like a miracle, this!'

'If it's true!'

'Then you don't think . . . '

'Noni, I don't know. Perhaps I'm just afraid to believe it because it's so important, not only to Philip but to us. I think you should see Herod — find out exactly what the position is.'

56

She smiled.

'That's exactly what I am doing. I'm seeing him at two-thirty.'

Bill glanced at his watch and slid to his feet.

'God, it's one fifteen! Have you had any lunch, darling?'

She shook her head.

'Nor have I. Come on, I'll take you out — there isn't time for a proper meal but we can get sandwiches at the Chequers.'

'But, Bill, someone might see us.'

Bill took her hands and pulled her to her feet.

'So what? There's no earthly reason why the hospital psychiatrist shouldn't be taking Mrs Brisbane to lunch. I'm fed up with having to hide you away, my darling. I don't even *feel* guilty. I feel as if our love is the only really good thing in the whole world.'

'I know!' She put her arms round his neck and pressed her face against his cheek in a child-like gesture which he was beginning to know. It touched him deeply each time she did it. 'It's not because we're underhand people, Bill. We're keeping quiet for Philip's sake — not for our own.'

'Yes! All the same, this time we're eating in public. Okay?'

He bent his head and kissed her. This time

she did not draw away from him and at the contact of their two bodies, desire replaced all other thoughts and caution too. Neither heard the door open behind them, nor saw the uniformed nurse standing there staring at them, her eyes wide with amazement.

Sarah Bristow coughed. It seemed the only thing to do. The couple sprang apart and stood staring back at her speechlessly.

'There's a message for you, Bill,' she said calmly. 'Mr Weeks wants you to see the little girl, Hilary MacPherson. He suspects the child is only pretending loss of memory so he'd be grateful if you could find time to go down to Ward Eight at five-thirty.'

Bill nodded. He felt like a small boy caught stealing, both ashamed and guilty.

'Look, Sarah . . . ' he began, but she interrupted him.

'I can be as blind as a bat when I want to be,' she said, smiling slightly. Then she turned and walked out of the room, closing the door behind her.

'Damn and blast!' He could see Noni was trembling. His own hand was unsteady.

'Don't worry, darling. I'm sure Sarah won't say anything. I *know* she won't. There's nothing to be afraid of.'

Noni shuddered.

'I feel . . . unclean!' she whispered.

'Darling, don't. It's difficult enough without our exaggerating things. I know Sarah Bristow. I can make up some story for her — tell her you came in here upset and you broke down and I was comforting you. She'll accept it.'

A little colour stole back into Noni's face. She looked suddenly much older.

'Of course, she's the one you . . . you and she . . . '

'Noni, we're just friends now. In a way, what happened once helps now. Sarah likes me and she has no cause to wish me any harm. I *know* we can trust her.'

'She's very striking!'

He smiled. Only a woman could notice the looks of the 'other woman' at a time like this.

His words to Noni had reassured him at the same time. Sarah was a good sort. Besides, she had always been far too involved in intrigues of her own to get any fun out of gossiping about other people. He'd have a word with her.

'Forget her, darling!' he said, taking Noni's arm and leading her to the door. 'We're going to have lunch.'

★　★　★

Sarah walked down the corridor towards her ward, her eyes thoughtful. What she had just witnessed had been something of a surprise. Bill Aden and Mrs Brisbane! And how long had *that* been going on? Of course, it might be the 'first time', but something in their combined embrace led her instinctively to suppose that they were already lovers. They'd been oblivious to her entry — lost in each other.

She was surprised. Bill had never got himself entangled with a married woman before. She could remember him saying to her that he didn't believe anything two human beings chose to do together was wrong unless it harmed someone else; and for that reason, he'd never let himself become involved with a married woman. He'd meant it, too. Bill was a curious person — he kept part of himself remote from his relationship with a woman and was always quite in control of himself. It wasn't so simple to do that if you were in love. And now? Was he in love with Mrs Brisbane? If so, the sooner he fell out of love the better. It would go pretty hard with him if anyone found out about it. The sympathy naturally would be with Philip Brisbane.

She had been to see Philip this morning, just as she had told Nancy she would. Pat, the night nurse, was a friend of hers and perfectly willing to let her slip in on the trumped-up excuse that she had a message for him. Philip had been eating his breakfast.

'You've got marmalade on your chin,' she'd told him.

'You're not the night nurse. You're . . . yes, you're Sister Bristow!'

He had been quick to recognise her voice.

'I thought I'd drop in and see how you were.'

'Nice of you. Thanks!' He'd wiped the marmalade off his chin with the napkin and said:

'Last time I put food over my face, my wife wiped it off for me. Perfectly capable of doing it myself. Much rather, too. Clever of you to know.'

'I'm a nurse, Mr Brisbane.'

He had laughed.

'Yes, and a very attractive one. Your voice . . . a blind person begins to notice such things. You have a very . . . very distinctive voice. One might say sympathetic but not pitying. Tell me, Sister, are you sorry for me?'

The question had taken her unawares. But she'd answered it truthfully.

'I'm sorry your career should have ended but I'm not sorry for you. I think you're a very strong person — that you'll rise above this sort of misfortune and make an equal success of something else. I might have felt sorry for a weaker man.'

She could tell by the expression on his face that he'd been pleased and flattered.

'You have courage, Mr Brisbane!' she'd said.

'Indeed I do, and you instill courage, Sister. By the way, what's your Christian name?'

'Sarah!'

'Huh, Biblical name — from the Hebrew, meaning princess or queen. Are you Jewish?'

'No, Mr Brisbane.'

'You can call me Philip if you like. After all, I'm a patient, not a surgeon right now!'

He'd laughed and she had laughed with him. Then Pat had put her head round the door to warn her that Matron was on her way and she'd left to go back to begin the day's work. She'd been wondering all day how she could wangle an exchange with Pat so she could be on Philip Brisbane's private room.

And now, she was even more anxious to be there. It would be interesting to meet Mrs Brisbane again, find out what she was really like. She'd looked rather young and frightened just now. A bit like Susan Mason. And that reminded her that Susan had twice been to see her that morning. The girl looked terrible and said she'd been feeling sick. She was terrified one of the other nurses would guess. She'd begged almost hysterically for Sarah to help her.

'If I do, I'm a damned fool!' she thought. 'If I don't the girl may kill herself. Nice choice I have. I suppose I *ought* to tell Matron!'

But somehow she couldn't bring herself to do that. She knew only too well what it would mean — dismissal for Susan and the damn doctor responsible getting off scotfree. It was so unfair. Everything was always in favour of the male sex. The females just had to stick by each other if they were going to keep their heads above water.

Sarah stopped dead in the corridor as an idea hit her. If Susan could get an abortion, all her problems would be over. No G.P. would recommend such an operation at this late stage, but Sarah was certain an abortion at a private clinic could be organised. However it would need money — there was the problem.

Suddenly the two things on her mind fused. Bill Aden, Susan Mason. Why shouldn't Bill provide the money — or some of it? The price of her silence! she thought wryly. But then she realized this was a form of blackmail. It *was* blackmail. She smiled. Not really — this would be between old friends and Bill could afford it. He was fairly well off with no wife or family to support and a high salary. A hundred pounds wouldn't be so much to him. And the young doctor responsible could supply what more was needed.

'I must think about it,' Sarah decided. She never acted without counting the consequences . . . 'I'll think about it tonight.'

4

Noni was not to see Mr Herod that afternoon. The surgeon was needed for an emergency case and a new appointment was made for Noni the following morning.

Because Philip had asked her to, she went back to visit him. The normal visiting hours had been waived for her because she was the wife of 'The Big Man'. Philip's reputation had helped him into his own hospital after the accident. Strings had been pulled hard at the Bedfordshire hospital where he had been taken directly after the car smash and Philip, through sheer force of will, Noni believed, had got where he wanted. It certainly made life easier for them all in many ways. She was able to live at home and see him whenever he wanted. The men treating him were all his personal colleagues.

He was still in excellent spirits when she went back into his room.

'That you, Noni?' he asked as she approached his bed. The sight of his bandaged eyes still shocked her each time she saw him.

'Who else?' she asked, trying to raise her

spirits to match his.

'Might have been that nurse of mine!' Philip's voice was amused. 'Attractive woman. Got her eye on me, I think. That make you jealous, Noni?'

'Yes, of course!' The lie came surprisingly easily. She sat down in the chair by his bed and wondered whether to touch his hand.

'Thought it might!' Philip said, pleased. 'I was asking my night nurse about our Sister Bristow. Quite a girl from all accounts.'

At Sister Bristow's name, the colour flamed hotly in Noni's cheeks. What had she to do with Philip? Fear made her hands tremble.

'Sister Bristow?'

'Oh, you wouldn't know her!' Philip said, his voice somehow managing to belittle her as if he thought she should have known what he was talking about. 'Red-haired piece. I remember seeing her about. Sexy's not the word.'

'Please, Philip!'

He was irritated.

'You really are the world's biggest prude!' he said, not troubling to conceal his annoyance. 'Mention sex to you and you behave like a silly little schoolgirl. Time you grew up a bit, my dear, and faced a few facts of life. As a matter of interest, I've been thinking about us. I've done quite a bit of thinking lying here with these damned bandages on my eyes. I think you ought to see Aden.'

'Aden?' The name was out in one horrified breath.

'Yes, *Aden*! Bill Aden, the psychiatrist. I'm serious about this, Noni. There's something very odd about your approach to sex — though you might well say 'Lack of enthusiasm for it.' Do you realize that it's three months since we . . . '

'Philip, please don't let's talk about that now.'

She might have saved her breath. Philip had started on one of his favourite hobby-horses — criticizing her.

'You can't deny it, Noni. A man knows when he isn't welcome in his wife's bed.'

'Then why do you insist on sharing it?' The words were out before she could control them.

Philip tapped his long thin fingers on the blanket.

'Because, my dear Noni, *I* happen to be normal and to have a normal husband's needs. It's your duty, as my wife, to oblige me.' He gave a little snort. 'You'd be the first one to turn on me in horrified disgust if I asked another woman to do what my wife wouldn't.'

'Philip, I've never refused . . . ' She broke off, knowing that this was no longer true. For six years she had tried to accept Philip as a lover with some outward display of pleasure. But since Bill, it had become impossible. The thought of Philip even kissing her was obnoxious — horrifying. Shortly before the accident, she had refused, for the first time in their married life, pleading an on-set of influenza.

'There's plenty of women anxious enough for it!' Philip was saying, not listening to what she had to say. 'Take that Sister Bristow, for example. I'll bet she'd give her right arm for what you turn your nose up at. Yes, there's something wrong with you and I think you owe it to me to have it put right. I'd like you to make an appointment to see Aden. He's supposed to be able to straighten people out and I imagine in your case, it *is* mental. There's nothing physically wrong with you — *I* know that.'

Noni tried to stop listening. This was Philip at his worst, crude, coarse and without a vestige of sensitivity. As to her seeing Bill — if Philip only knew . . .

'You should get on all right with Aden — quite a ladies' man, I believe. Tell him I sent you and no doubt he'll give you extra time and attention . . . '

'Philip, I ought to leave now. I . . . I have some shopping to do.'

But he reached out and at the second attempt, caught her wrist.

'Damn the shopping!' he said. 'I want you with me.' His voice became softer as his fingers felt the smooth velvet texture of the skin on her inner arm. 'I may not be able to see you, but by God, I can feel you, Noni. You're a damned attractive woman. And what's more, it may not be so long before I can take a real good *look* at you. You can't believe how much Herod has cheered me up. The bloody fool said I was stone blind when I first saw him. But I'm not — no, indeed. There's some sight remaining and he can operate. I wormed that out of him this morning though it took me long enough. But I know what's wrong with him — he's afraid of raising false hopes. Taken his line myself in the past with a too-optimistic patient. Can't blame him, really . . . '

Her mind was no longer following him. She was trying to think out this new crazy idea of Philip's that she should see Bill. Surely he couldn't be serious. He *couldn't*. But Philip was capable of such an idea. It simply would never occur to him that her lack of enthusiasm for that side of her married life was his fault. How strange that they should never have discussed this before. Philip had never complained; had appeared to take it for granted that everything was straightforward because she had never complained either. And all this time he had known something was wrong and only *now* suggested they do something about it. Was it just coincidence that he'd suddenly awakened to some home truths at the same time *she* had discovered there was so much more to loving than just sex? She hadn't known before Bill, how truly beautiful the act could be. She had been only dimly aware of distaste, or dread for something she should have been able to enjoy. If Philip had spoken so openly about it before, she would have believed him for she, too, thought that there was something wrong with her that she could not enjoy this side of her marriage. Now she knew that it wasn't her fault. All Philip's sensitivity was centred in his finger tips, there was none left for his heart; all his skill lay in dissecting the human body; there was none left for loving it. For him it had meant no more than assuaging a thirst or satisfying an appetite. And he had failed to understand why she was not hungry, too.

'Are you listening to me? Dash it all, Noni, you could trouble to answer me. Have you or have you not spoken to Herod?'

70

'No. No, I haven't!'

'Damn! Then you can't confirm the fact that I may be okay for my work eventually. I don't care how long it takes — I know some of these post-operative cases need a hell of a long convalescence. I can stick that — so long as I can see well enough to operate at the end of it. I was lucky my hands weren't injured. The leg's mending pretty well.'

Noni felt as if her mind was in a whirlpool — thoughts and fears swirling round one another so fast that it was difficult to grab and hold onto one single one. Now, it seemed, Philip was no longer one hundred per cent certain that Mr Herod could operate successfully. This morning, he'd left no room for doubt. What was the truth? It was so terribly important for all their sakes. For each of the three of them — Philip, Bill, herself — a whole life's happiness was at stake.

Philip began to question her about affairs at home. For a few moments, they were united in the arrangement of domestic matters. Philip had a clear, concise brain and could tackle the day to day problems of living with clear-cut authority. Then he dictated a letter to his elderly parents living in Northumberland. Noni could not do short-hand and he became impatient with her slowness in writing.

'Can't you go any faster?' he asked irritably. If he had not been ill, she might have lost her temper with him. But the pent-up emotions of the last hour in his company had to have their outlet somewhere. She burst into tears. Philip, far from regretting his lack of consideration, became more irritable.

'Do take a grip on yourself, Noni. This whole business of my accident seems to have knocked you to pieces. There'd be some excuse if I were the one who was cracking up.'

'I'm sorry, Philip. I — I'm afraid things have been getting me down.'

'Well, stop feeling sorry for yourself. And for pity's sake, stop being sorry for me.' He gave a sudden laugh. 'Rather clever that — what? 'For pity's sake.' A play on words. Get it, Noni?'

For the first time in her married life, Noni discovered a vital truth about Philip — he was really just a child. One was misled into believing that here was a brilliant mature man because he was brilliant *in his own field of work*. But beyond that, he understood little or nothing. It was possible to understand how this could have happened. He'd wanted to be a surgeon since he was a small boy at grammar school dissecting frogs for the first time in the school lab. He'd told her the story

72

of how he had suddenly known what he wanted to do with his life — to be. From that moment, he had studied and worked to this one end. Any subject outside his chosen profession had not the slightest interest for him. He learned only what he must in order to pass O levels; then dropped the subjects not required for A level passes into Edinburgh University. And so the years of his life had passed into this one narrow channel, leaving him at the core of his being still the grammar school boy with an outward veneer of sophistication.

This was Philip Brisbane — one of the most highly respected men in surgery. All their friends were in the medical profession and so his ignorance of life beyond the hospital was never questioned. At their dinner parties, talk was always of new techniques, new discoveries, past triumphs or failures. The wives tended to group together discussing domestic matters, their children if they had any, accepting that their husbands preferred to bring their 'office' lives to the dinner table. There had been many such evenings when Noni had felt so bored she wanted to scream. There were so many other vital topics of conversation — politics, art, music, the theatre, books. She herself read avidly on an enormous variety of subjects

— novels, autobiographies, history, travel. Philip's reading matter stayed rigidly grooved. No wonder, then, that he had not grown up.

Against her will, the comparison between Philip, her husband, and Bill, the man she loved, was forcing itself to the forefront of her mind. In all their stolen hours together, she had never heard Bill discuss his patients, his cases. Their conversations ranged over the widest fields, one casual word leading them into fresh exchanges of ideas and opinions. To be with Bill meant to have one's mind endlessly stimulated and excited. She had found herself discussing things she had until then only thought of. As if Bill had released a dam, they rushed from her, tumbling over one another in confusion until Bill took each one and enlarged it, clarified it, weighed it until they found what they believed to be the truth of the matter.

'There's a new *Lancet* somewhere on the bed table,' Philip was saying. 'You might read it to me, Noni. I mustn't let myself slip behind with these things.'

She found the magazine but they were interrupted by the day nurse — the young Jamaican girl Noni had begun to know and to like. Philip, however, seemed to have a dislike for the girl.

'It's not that I'm prejudiced,' he said,

forgetting the *Lancet* while he drank his tea. 'One just doesn't like the idea of having inferior nurses.'

'But, Philip, why should she be inferior? From all I've heard, these West Indians are marvellous. This one certainly seems very efficient.'

'I'm not denying they have their uses, especially when we can't get enough white girls into the jobs. But I won't have one in the theatre when I'm operating and what's more, Matron knows it.'

'You're referring to that young girl from Trinidad?'

Noni remembered Philip's account of the incident. He'd told her one evening at dinner. He'd been operating on a little girl of three and the child had died. The Trinidadian nurse had burst into tears.

Noni had tried to defend her. She was very young — it was her first day in the theatre. If she had a fault, it was only that of being too soft-hearted. But Philip would have none of it. He couldn't — or wouldn't — be fair. No matter how he might argue that it was not the case, he had a strong colour prejudice and it became such a bone of contention between them that Noni avoided the subject whenever she could.

Philip was too exacting. He demanded the

highest standards of efficiency from everyone who worked for him or around him and this had frequently made him many near enemies and lost him a number of potential friends. He might have been criticized for this rigid attitude were it not for the fact that he was above reproach himself . . . where his work was concerned; and since his private life was really only a continuation of his work, that, too, remained above reproach. Philip would never have one drink too many because it could affect his operating next day. He kept to an unvaried routine for sleep; watched his diet carefully, believing that only a man in the best of health was fit for the heavy demands of his job. His morals, too, enabled him to fall heavily onto those who erred. Philip never wandered from the marriage bed. He never had to. Noni was there when he wanted her. He would not accept that for some people, marriage had failed.

'A married man who messes around with other women is risking his good name,' Philip had declared stoutly. 'For a doctor, that's too high a price for a moment's fun.'

'Fun!' Noni had echoed. 'Maybe it's love, Philip.'

'Love! Lot of romantic hoo-hah. What a man wants when he takes a woman to bed isn't love, my dear girl, whatever fancy name he likes to give it.'

He'd spent half an hour going into the proof of what he was saying. He had in the course of his career, handled every part of the human body. Each part had its particular reason for being there, its uses. Like mathematics, one and one made two. A heart was filled with blood and valves and arteries — there wasn't an ounce of love to be seen. But sex — that made sense. Nature intended man to want woman and woman to desire man. One and one make two. Same with the brain although Philip granted there was a lot more to be discovered about the human brain.

'But mark my words, Noni, you won't find a container for this 'love' you and the 'telly' and those books you read keep talking about.'

Perhaps that occasion marked the day she had first realized that she did not love Philip — had never loved him. His own biological explanation had struck home. What she had felt for him could be given other names — respect, admiration, interest and a few brief moments of ordinary human womanly desire. But she had never loved him. Nor had he ever loved her.

Because of her strict upbringing, Noni was bound by conventions and morality. She did not question then that she must not go through life without this great experience of loving and being loved; that she should try to find an alternative life partner to Philip; start seeking for someone to love. She accepted that because she had made a mistake and married the wrong man, it must be her lot to remain in the prison of her own making and try to make their relationship as good a thing as possible. She was resigned, with only odd moments of depression and despair, to the hollowness of her existence, until the day she met Bill . . .

Thank heaven Philip had, for the moment anyway, forgotten his idea of Bill taking her on as his patient! That would be truly ironic. How she hated the necessity for this deceit! If only she could say now: *Philip, forgive me but I've fallen in love with Bill. Please give me a divorce. We want to be married.*

This was what she had intended doing after those few brief days and nights when she had first gone away with Bill. The idea of an 'intrigue on the side' appalled her and Bill had agreed. She had meant to ask Philip at the very first opportunity to set her free. But the truth was that she was afraid of him and more afraid that he would refuse a divorce. Then Philip had himself gone away to a medical conference in Scotland and there had been no chance. Then on the way back — the accident — and what might have been so simple and straightforward had become virtually an impossibility.

She wondered how long she could stand this strain . . . the not knowing what the future held. It might be weeks now before they could be sure the operation on Philip's eyes was a success. Weeks of not knowing; of trying to pretend to Philip that all was the same between them as it ever had been.

She could be grateful now, for the first time in her life, for Philip's lack of sensitivity; lack of curiosity about her. He never said, as Bill did: *What are you thinking, Noni?* He wasn't really at all interested in her except as a reflection of himself; a provider of his creature comforts and needs. He was far too easy to deceive. It would be very easy, especially now whilst Philip was confined to a hospital bed, to take time off to be with Bill. But now, because of the circumstances, she couldn't. 'Stealing from a blind man.' How apt the saying was in her case. She hated herself because she knew she was powerless to say *No* to Bill once he took her in his arms. Somehow she must make him understand that this feeling of guilt towards Philip would end up ruining their happiness. *They had* to wait until Philip was better. There could be no more dangerous moments like the one at

79

lunch time in Bill's office. Would that nurse say anything to anyone? Just suppose word were to get back to Philip? Would he be horrified? Hurt? *Or might he not even mind?*

As if in direct answer to the perilous thoughts, Philip said out of the blue:

'Take this tray off my bed, will you, Noni? You know, I'm going to need you much more than I have in the past — for a while anyway. I'd like you to arrange the domestic routine so you can be here with me at least four or five hours a day. Until I can see to write my own letters, I'll need to dictate everything. Then there's the reading — you can keep me up to date with that. It's a good thing we have a joint account so you can sign cheques. Yes, you'll have to reckon on being my secretary as well as my wife. Give you something to do.'

'I'll come as often as I can, Philip!' she promised. Her heart sank at the thought of hours alone with Philip when her nerves were so tensed — her emotions so confused. But she couldn't refuse.

The nurse came in, this time with a thermometer.

'Evening round already?' Philip asked. Noni got up to leave. She smiled at the nurse, in some odd way trying to compensate for Philip's feelings towards the girl.

'I'll see you tomorrow, Philip.' She stooped

and touched his cheeks with her lips. The presence of the nurse made the lack of a fuller expression of affection excusable.

He gave her a list of things he wished her to bring next day. Then she was out of his room, her back to the door, her heart beating as if she were an escaped prisoner. She tried to control her feelings of relief. It seemed so terrible to be glad to leave one's husband alone in a hospital room.

A doctor in a white coat came down the corridor towards her. She turned quickly and hurried off towards the lift. She hoped she would not run into anyone she knew. All she wanted was to get home and be by herself.

No one spoke to her as she hurried out of the main doors towards the car park. It was dark already and a thin cold wind sent a scurry of leaves past her feet. Autumn — soon it would be winter.

There were not many cars left in the parking lot. Hers was on the extreme left. As she opened the driver's door, she saw the faint outlines of a man's figure in the passenger seat and fear shot through her. Then Bill's voice said:

'Get in, darling. I've been waiting for hours!'

She had no strength left to argue with him; to tell him he shouldn't be there in the car with her; that people might see them together. Besides, she was glad to see him. She wanted desperately to unload some of the burden onto his shoulders.

She started the car and switched on the headlights. At the main gates, the porter called 'Good night!' and then they were driving away from the hospital. Bill lent forward and switched on the panel light. In the faint glow, she could discern his profile. The tension was going, leaving her legs trembling.

'Stop here, on the left!' Bill said curtly. 'I'll drive.'

They changed places and Bill restarted the car. He switched on the heater and warmth began to steal back into her limbs. For a mile or two he drove in silence. Then he pulled up again beside a phone box.

'That's for you to ring home, Noni. Tell Mrs Reeves or whatever that you'll be out to dinner. I'm taking you back to my flat.'

'Bill, no!'

'Darling!' His voice was suddenly very gentle. He might have been speaking to a child. 'I'm not going to make love to you. I know how you're feeling about Philip. I've felt it, too, though not so deeply as you. We won't even kiss if you don't want to. But we do have to talk.'

'What will I say to Mrs Reeves? And suppose Philip phones?'

'So you are out to dinner — with me. Look, darling, your guilty conscience is confusing matters. Suppose we meant nothing at all to each other and we'd run into one another at the car park. What could be more natural than that knowing you've been having a hard time of it, I should ask you out to dinner? I doubt if Philip would object.'

She gave a wry little laugh.

'Far from it. He has suggested that I consult you professionally, Bill.'

'Consult me? Whatever for?'

He caught sight of her chalk-white face and said firmly:

'No, don't tell me now. Later. Go and phone Mrs Reeves.'

She let him take charge with an immense feeling of relief. There was no need to battle on alone. She could trust Bill.

Half an hour later, she was curled up in his big leather armchair in front of the electric fire. Bill sat on the floor, his back against her legs, his arm across her lap. In one hand she held a gin and tonic, the other Bill held tightly in his own across his shoulder.

'Feeling better, sweetheart?'

'Yes! How wonderful you always are to me. I'm afraid I love you very much, Bill.'

'Don't be afraid.' Despite its soft tone, his voice was serious.

'Fear is the undoing of most of my patients. One should try never to be afraid . . . of pain, sorrow, dying, living. Fear is always anticipatory. It means one suffers all the bad things twice, once being afraid beforehand and once when the worst happens.'

'That's so easy to say, Bill. I *am* afraid . . . afraid Philip isn't going to get better; afraid we shall lose each other; afraid that Sister Bristow will gossip; afraid Philip will find out I don't love him.'

'I know, Noni. But it's best to stamp as hard as you can when a fear raises its ugly head. *Que sera, sera.* What will be will be. There isn't really so much we can do about it, is there?'

'You mean, we have no choices to make?'

'Well, have we, my darling? If you were not you and I were not me, maybe we could decide to run off together whatever happens to Philip. But I don't think I could and I know *you* couldn't. So because we are us, we haven't a choice.'

Once again, unaccustomed tears were pouring down her cheeks. She put down her drink and tried to brush them away with the back of her hand, but not before Bill noticed them. He turned quickly, kneeling in front of her, his cheek pressed to hers.

'Darling Noni, don't cry, my love. Don't cry!'

'It's b . . . because you're s . . . so nice!' She essayed a smile which trembled on her lips. Bill said:

'You're the first woman I've known who still looks beautiful when she cries!'

'Oh, Bill!' She closed her eyes and reached for his hand. This way, close, close against him, fear *was* gone. Everything was safe and warm and beautiful and *right*.

'We belong to one another!' she whispered.

'Yes, we belong!'

This time he drew away and getting to his feet, walked across the room to pour out another drink for himself. The moment was almost more than he could bear. This was no ordinary casual love affair. This was far deeper and reached into the very depth of his soul. Noni was in his very being — a part of him. If he lost her now, she would still be with him all the rest of his life. He would never be able to find this strange wonderful affinity with another woman. He wondered if Noni's love for him could possibly go as deep. It seemed as if no one could love another human being *more* than he loved her.

He stared at the back of her fair head and fear and tenderness mingled in equal parts. If he could, he would protect her from everything that threatened her happiness. If he had the right, he would live only to bring wonder and beauty into her life. As things stood, it might have been better for her if they'd never had that dance which had been the beginning of love for them both.

He dared not stay too close to her. The temptation to make love to her was too over-powering and he knew that she did not wish to violate her sense of fair play towards her husband. It was all the harder because there was nothing to stop them except their own consciences . . .

'Noni, did Philip give you any fresh clues as to his chances?'

'No! But I'm afraid, Bill. He seemed to expect me to be able to confirm Herod's opinion. He was bitterly disappointed because I hadn't been able to talk to Herod this afternoon as we expected. This morning, Philip sounded so definite. This afternoon, he was confident enough and yet — why should he want so much to hear what Herod says to me? At the same time, he was full of plans for the future. You know — *'when I'm okay again'*; *'until I can see'*; the kind of remark that indicates he expects the operation to take place and to be a success.'

Bill nodded.

'Could be all wishful thinking! God, how nerve-racking this is. I simply can't contemplate a world without you now, darling. I just can't. This afternoon was too frightful. I don't think I can have helped my poor patients one whit. All the time I was thinking about us — our chances and how I couldn't bear it if I had to lose you.'

She stared up at him from large, frightened eyes.

'Bill, you mustn't depend on me. You'll have to be strong enough for both of us. I don't know what I'd do if I thought you were going to be unhappy. But you wouldn't . . . you'd forget me, marry someone else. You were quite happy before . . . '

'Yes, *before*!' he broke in roughly. 'As a beggar may be content until he meets his first rich man. I didn't realize what it could mean to love and be loved by a woman like you, Noni. You know already that there were several affairs in my past but it isn't fair even to think of them in the same context. This time sex is only a very small part of all I feel for you. Of course I'm attracted to you — *that* side of things was perfect for both of us, wasn't it? But it's you, Noni, what lies deep down inside your heart; the thoughts you are thinking; your companionship — these are what I want most. I love you so very, very much.'

'It couldn't be more than I love you. I'd give my life for you, Bill, without a second thought. When I read that in books I used to smile, thinking how dramatic it sounded and how unreal it really was. But it's true — I don't think I would hesitate for a moment. You are more precious to me than anything or anyone in the world.'

Silence — painful and complete, fell between them as each realized at the same moment that this was not, after all, true. Philip came first — not from love but from a moral duty which she could not ignore. In the last resort, duty — or pity, came before Bill's happiness, just as it had to come before her own.

Because the moment was so tense, he knew he must break it somehow.

'I'm going to fix you something to eat, my love,' he said as casually as he could. 'I've a steak in the fridge. Let's have that with some frozen peas. Be all right for you?'

'I'll cook it.' She was on her feet. 'Let me, Bill. I've never cooked you a meal. I'd like to do it.'

'We'll do it together.'

She followed him into the tiny kitchen, fighting hard against the depressing sense of impending loss. This was what marriage to

Bill *could* mean — cooking meals together, sharing everything. And it might never be possible.

She tried to push the ugly thought out of her mind. Bill had told her that fear of the future only meant suffering everything twice. She must make this one of the golden, precious moments of time to be treasured in her memory for the years to come. She must not spoil the present by thinking of the future.

But hours later, when she had driven home and was alone in bed, trying desperately to find the solace of sleep, the future came pressing in on her, tormenting her with its emptiness, its futility, its loneliness. Such was marriage with Philip. It always had been and she could not believe that it could ever be any different because that was the way Philip was and she was. They were just not made to satisfy each other's needs.

Philip ought never to have married at all. He was really married to his profession and had time and thought for little else. He did not even have the usual male hobbies such as golf or tennis. Since she was not a doctor herself, there was absolutely nothing in his life she could share — except his bed and that was a side of her marriage she dared not think about. To sleep with Philip now was an impossibility. Somehow she would have to have her own room if their married life were to continue. Philip would not understand and she couldn't explain to him — but she couldn't go back to the old passive acceptance of what she had thought of as her duty. That had only been possible before she had fallen in love with Bill and discovered what physical love was meant to be. It amazed her now to think that Philip had been satisfied. He'd complained about her lack of what he called 'enthusiasm' but surely it wasn't possible that he was totally ignorant of how love between a man and wife could be?

But even as the thought went through her mind, she knew that it *was* possible. Philip didn't believe in love. He only believed in sex.

She felt hot and restless as she tossed and turned between the sheets, longing for sleep that would not come. Stronger than her will, the memory of their goodnight kiss before she left Bill's flat, forced itself into her mind. There had been a desperate fight against their helpless desire for closer contact. With their mouths and bodies moulded together, passion had flamed so violently in each of them that Noni would have forgotten all her newly-made vows had Bill not managed somehow to keep control of himself. Now she was half-grateful to Bill and at the same time uncertain of the sense behind her insistence that they should not make love again until they knew Philip was all right. In the darkness alone and desperately frustrated, she asked herself if she was making matters worse rather than better. Soon there might not be a chance to make love — Bill might be far away, out of her life, out of reach for ever. Wasn't it plain madness not to take what they could while they could? What Philip did not know couldn't hurt him. They would be harming no one — only their own consciences. And they were already facing the possibility of giving up so much for Philip's happiness. Must they give up these few brief moments of happiness, too?

Suddenly she remembered the note left by Mrs Reeves, the cook.

'I hope you had a pleasant dinner, Mrs Brisbane, dear. It will have done you good this terribly worrying time. I've left a hot drink in the thermos.'

Remembering, she was glad after all, that the evening had not ended in adultery. How could she face Mrs Reeves at breakfast with her kindly questions and concern, knowing that she had been cheating a blind man . . . a blind man . . .

'No!' The word sprang from her lips into the darkness. She covered her face with her hands. 'Dear God, let him see again; not just for my sake and Bill's, but for his too. Dear God, Please!'

She fell asleep before she had completed her prayers.

5

'I'm extremely sorry, Mrs Brisbane. I thought I had made it absolutely clear to you when we last discussed your husband's case, that he would never be able to operate again.'

Noni looked at the grey-haired bespectacled man who was so sympathetically dealing out a second blow and tried to steady her voice.

'Yes, you did, Mr Herod. But Philip told me you'd seen him yesterday and said you could operate. He . . . he said things were not as bad as you had at first feared.'

'That is perfectly true, Mrs Brisbane. I don't know quite how your husband could have misunderstood what I said. There is *some* residual vision, a very, very small percentage in *one* eye. I told him I thought I could operate and improve this. I'm practically certain that this can be done. But to all intents and purposes, Mrs Brisbane — forgive me for talking so bluntly — your husband will remain a blind man. He will not be able to see to read, for instance. He might, if the operation is successful, be able to discern vague shadows such as a heavy object of furniture, but he wouldn't be able to do more than guess what the object was. That, I'm afraid is the unpalatable truth.'

He took off his glasses and wiped them with an uneasy concentration.

'I just cannot understand how he took it that I said I *could* restore his sight. As you can readily understand, I took great pains *not* to raise his hopes.'

Noni felt her heart hammering so fiercely that she wondered if the man opposite could hear it. Her only thought as yet was:

'Poor Philip. *Poor, poor Philip*!' But slowly the agonizing truth was boring its way into her consciousness — that there was no hope for Bill and herself either. They were all doomed by Mr Herod's prognosis.

'I'm so sorry, Mrs Brisbane. Naturally, when you asked to see me yesterday, I had no idea that this misunderstanding had occurred. I had better go and see your husband myself — unless, of course, you feel that you . . . ?'

'No, no!' She reined in her voice and, on a lower key, said: 'No, you tell him, please. I don't want to be the one to break this news.'

'Of course. But I expect you will want to go into him afterwards. Offer him what comfort and sympathy you can. You're going to mean a great deal to him now, Mrs Brisbane. Your love and care and help will be the main bulwark against his blindness. A great tragedy — a very great tragedy indeed. You have my personal as well as my professional sympathy, Mrs Brisbane. I'm afraid this has been a shock to you. May I suggest you go and have a strong cup of tea — get yourself quite under control before you go to see your husband.'

'Quite under control, quite under control, quite . . . ' The words reiterated meaninglessly as she found her way to the canteen near the out-patients waiting hall, and obediently drank two cups of strong, sweet tea. Someone spoke to her and she replied without actually taking in the question.

Suddenly, she knew that she must go to Philip. Whatever shock she must be feeling, it would be a hundred times worse for him. How selfish she was being even to consider herself.

She hurried along the corridor and took the lift up to the third floor. Outside Philip's room she all but collided with Sister Bristow. Sarah put out a steadying hand. Her glance at Noni's face was professional. She guessed that Mrs Brisbane had already heard what Mr Herod had just been telling her!

'Steady now! Sure you're okay?'

'Yes, thank you! It's all right for me to go in?'

Sarah nodded and stood watching as Noni opened the door of her husband's room and disappeared inside.

She frowned. Something didn't quite add up here. If ever a woman looked deeply upset, it was Noni Brisbane. Sarah had seen with her own eyes that same woman in Bill's arms, her eyes closed, her whole body expressing love. Yet now it seemed as if she might, after all, still love her husband. Was she then one of those spoilt rich women who played around outside marriage just for the hell of it, but needed a shock like this to make her realize she still loved her husband after all?

Standing as she was, lost in thought, she became an unwitting eavesdropper. Philip Brisbane's voice was raised in anger:

' . . . you stop saying you're sorry. I'm not asking you to be sorry for me. I'm going to get another opinion. You don't think I'll let the matter rest here, do you?'

There was an indistinguishable murmur and then Philip's voice.

'Damn Herod. Let him say what he wants. *I* know what he told me yesterday. I'm not deaf — or a fool. And I don't need you to tell me the different line he's taking today . . . '

Sarah remained hesitating. It was not her business to interfere between husband and wife in private conversation. On the other hand, Mr Brisbane was her patient and he had just had a severe shock. If he were sufficiently violently disturbed he might even try to get out of bed . . .

She opened the door and said calmly:

'Did you ring, Mr Brisbane?'

'No, I didn't, damn it! But since you're here, Sister, you can do something for me.'

'Yes, of course, sir.'

Her cool voice had the desired effect of calming him.

'Get Harvey up here at once. I want to see him immediately.'

'I'll see if he can be found, sir.' She took a quick professional look at Noni's chalk white face and said: 'As I'm not permitted to leave this floor whilst I'm on duty, perhaps you could spare Mrs Brisbane?'

'Yes, go on with Sister, Noni!' Philip ordered impatiently. 'And I hope the man hasn't left the hospital. I'm going to have a talk with him if it's the last thing I do.'

Outside his room, Noni drew in a deep breath and let it out again. Her legs were trembling.

'Come on!' Sarah said gently. 'You can take a pew in my room. I can get hold of Mr Harvey on the 'phone.'

Noni followed Sarah into the small room where the nurse in charge kept her records.

There was a desk and chair, a prescription cupboard and little else.

'Thank you!' she said simply. 'I just don't seem to have the knack of calming him.'

'Everything is difficult for your husband at the moment. He's been used to complete independence and now he is utterly dependent; he's used to giving orders and not taking them, and he's used to dishing out verdicts on cases and not receiving them. Doctors are always hopeless patients. One just has to be brisk and firm.'

'But I can't be . . . I'm so *sorry* for him!' Noni whispered. 'He . . . he seems to resent my sympathy.'

'Naturally. He's a very proud man!'

Noni looked up, surprised.

'Of course, you know him very well!' she said. 'I suppose my husband as a man is not so different from my husband, the surgeon.'

'Practically no difference at all at a shrewd guess!' murmured Sarah, reaching for the phone.

She hadn't been sure until now how she felt about Mrs Brisbane. There'd been a medley of feelings, really. Envy when she'd seen her round the hospital in the old days — beautifully groomed and dressed and very much the attractive young wife of The Big

Man; jealousy because Noni was pretty in an utterly feminine way that could never be Sarah's; then dislike when she'd caught her in Bill's office, cheating on a blind man. Now, suddenly, she felt only pity and a strange sympathy. It was all too obvious that Noni was scared stiff of her husband when he flew off the handle. She was too soft-hearted to fight back which was what he needed. A woman to argue back at him would have given him a chance to work off some of his aggressiveness against Fate. Noni Brisbane wasn't the arguing type. She'd get caught up in situations and not know how to extricate herself.

She put through her call to Matron, explaining briefly what had happened and that her patient wished to see Mr Harvey at once if it was possible. Then she turned back to Noni.

'I expect you'd like a cup of tea!' she said gently.

For the first time in hours, Noni smiled.

'Everyone seems to prescribe tea for me today. I couldn't drink another cup. Thanks all the same.'

'Are you in love with Bill?'

Both women blushed. Sarah had not meant to ask the question. It had slipped out, taking Noni as well as herself off guard.

99

'No, don't answer that — unless you want to!'

Noni could not find words for a moment. Then she prevaricated.

'You were in love with him once, weren't you?'

Sarah shrugged her shoulders.

'In love? I wonder what that really means. I suppose I was, after a fashion. But he certainly wasn't in love with me. So that's one thing you don't have to worry about. It was all over ages ago anyway.'

'Yes, Bill told me!'

Somehow the relief of being able to mention his name outweighed the need for caution.

'Well, that's cleared up then. I always think it would make life so much easier if everyone were to be completely honest with everyone else.'

'Yes, but it isn't always possible!' Noni replied. 'Sometimes there are circumstances . . . well, which make it impossible to admit the truth.'

Again Sarah shrugged her shoulders.

'If I were in love,' she said quietly, 'and the man loved me, I wouldn't let anything or anyone stand between us. I believe real love is a pretty rare thing.'

'So she knows the truth!' Noni thought.

She wasn't sure how Sarah could know but there was little doubt that she did.

'I would never do anything to hurt my husband!' she said. 'Not now he has been so terribly hurt by a fate which could not have struck more cruelly.'

'All the same, pity and noble sacrifices and the like aren't going to be much use to a man like him.'

Noni was silent. These were Bill's words and yet she could not endorse them. Even if she couldn't give Philip love, she could make life easier and happier for him, encourage him to begin a new life somehow. She could find new *interests* for him.

Quite suddenly she realized that she was caught in a grip of the strangest situation — a discussion about her private life with a woman who was little more than a complete stranger to her. She must be out of her mind.

'I really don't know what we are talking about,' she said, standing up and trying to appear casual and indifferent. 'If you don't mind, Sister, I prefer to forget this conversation and I'd be grateful if you'd do the same. I'm going home now. If Mr Brisbane should ask for me, will you tell him I wasn't feeling too well and he can ring me at home?'

'Yes, of course!'

When Noni had departed, Sarah gave that

characteristic shrug of her shoulders. She could confidently go and pay a visit to Bill and extract some money from him. He could well afford it and poor little Susan was desperate. She'd get relieved for an early lunch and pop in to his office after his last patient.

'Poor old Bill!' she thought. But it didn't stop her going in to see him.

* * *

'Hullo, Bill!'

He looked up from his desk where he had been awaiting the last of the morning's patients and saw Sarah Bristow. For a second, an uneasy guilt robbed him of his customary composure.

'May I sit down?'

'Yes, of course!'

She looked, as always, very neat in her nurse's uniform. The little starched cap covered only part of her magnificent red hair. There was no doubt about it, Sarah was a handsome woman.

'What can I do for you, Sarah?'

Calmly, she took out a packet of cigarettes from her apron pocket, and lit one. She seemed in no hurry to open the conversation.

'I want some help, Bill,' she said. 'Financial help!'

Bill's face darkened. His relationship with Sarah was a slightly odd one. On duty they were Mr Aden and Sister Bristow, but off duty they called one another by their Christian names. After their affair ended they had maintained a casual friendship which in no way interfered with their work in the hospital. Occasionally, if he ran into her in the nearby pub, he would stand her a drink. Once in a while they would meet in the canteen. Nothing more.

'I need a hundred pounds!'

'But I can't . . . ' Bill began, and then broke off. What on earth could Sarah need such a sum of money for? And why ask *him*?

'What for?' he asked bluntly.

'Not for myself. One of the girls is in trouble. She has to have the money and I've none to give her. I thought you might help.'

'But why me?' Bill asked, more puzzled than ever. 'Do I know the girl? And what kind of trouble?'

'The usual. As for you knowing the girl, I rather doubt it.'

'Then why should I give her money?'

'Why not?' Sarah retorted, her tone quite pleasant but with an undertone of firmness that made it impossible for Bill to write this off as a joke. 'You should understand the difficulties facing a girl with no money and no one to help her. Someone's got to. She can't have the baby.'

Bill tried to fathom Sarah's reasoning. If he didn't know the girl, why involve him? Besides, he simply could not and would not become involved with late abortions.

'Can't the man help?'

'A little — but not enough. She needs more.'

'Am I to know her name?'

'No! She's just one of the younger nurses. The father is a fourth-year student so you can see there isn't much cash floating round.'

'I see! All the same, Sarah, I would as soon not be involved in any way.'

'I'm sure you would rather stay out of it. But I don't know anyone else to ask. And I thought you might be in a sympathetic mood.'

'And what makes you think that I . . . ' Once more he broke off in mid-sentence. His quick brain had readily guessed at the hidden barb behind Sarah's words. She was referring to his affair with Noni . . .

'Are you blackmailing me, Sarah?'

This time it was Sarah's turn to look confused and uncertain. But she held his gaze as she replied.

'I don't see why you have to make it sound so unattractive. I'm a friend asking a friend for help. We are friends, aren't we, Bill?'

He looked away from her and down at his blotter. He wondered if he dare refuse help. She might go to Philip — not that she had any proof of guilt between Noni and him — but she could plant a few ugly suspicions in his mind. *But would she?* Was Sarah, whom he knew and had always rather liked, capable of such behaviour?

As if guessing his thoughts, Sarah said flatly:

'I've been transferred to Mr Brisbane's floor.'

'I see!' Now he could no longer doubt the reason for Sarah's visit. She wanted the price of her silence! It *was* blackmail, whatever she might like to call it.

'Well, will you help, Bill?'

'I'd much prefer not to become involved!' he said slowly.

'That I can understand. We all prefer not to become involved when there's a hint of trouble on the horizon. Unfortunately, it isn't always easy to stay free of involvements, is it? People have an unfortunate way of falling in love and that complicates life.'

'Sarah, *if* I'm to help, and I'm not promising, I'd like to know exactly what the money is for. *You're* not the one in trouble, are you? You know I'd be more than willing to help if you . . . '

For the first time, her face softened.

'No, it's not me. The reason I gave you is perfectly genuine, thanks all the same, Bill. But the poor kid is desperate. She's hysterical enough to try to kill herself if she can't see any other way out. A hundred pounds for a life isn't much, is it? I wouldn't be asking you if I had as much myself.'

'Why can't this girl have her baby? The D.H.S.S. will help her financially and she could get the child adopted.'

'You don't know what you're talking about, Bill. Matron would find out — and what kind of reference do you think the girl would get so that she could go on nursing after it's all over — and that's assuming she could support herself after she had the baby. Her parents would disown her and she has two schoolgirl sisters whose lives might also become affected if the whole thing came out. There is really only one choice, Bill — abortion. But she'll need money. You'll have to take my word for all this. I can't offer you proof.'

'And where do you stand in all this?'

Sarah gave an enigmatic smile.

'Loco parentis, perhaps? Call it my soft

106

heart. I just think a kid like that ought not to have all the hard knocks that are going. Or say I'm against injustice, if you like. As you may remember, I've a bit of an obsession about the way the scales are always weighted in favour of the man.'

'Late abortions can be dangerous,' Bill said thoughtfully. 'And psychologically they can be very damaging.'

'I don't want to argue the ethics of the case. I just want to know if you'll help?'

'And if I don't?'

Sarah hesitated. Both knew what her unspoken reply would be — a threat to tell Mr Brisbane what she had walked in on this time yesterday in Bill's office.

'I'd prefer not to think of that because I think you will help, won't you? For old time's sake?'

He knew he had no choice. Noni would be out of her mind with worry if she thought Sarah might gossip to Brisbane. And as Sarah was now Brisbane's nurse, they would be in constant danger. He didn't think she would talk, but she might.

He realized he was falling into the trap open to all who allowed themselves to be blackmailed. Even if he gave Sarah the money she asked for, there was still no guarantee she would keep quiet. And she could assume from his willingness to pay that he and Noni were admitting their guilt. Moreover, she could come back for more money.

Sarah stood up.

'Think about it,' she said bluntly. 'You may like to discuss it with Mrs Brisbane. I'll drop in again some time tomorrow.'

Ignoring his flushed, angry face, she turned and left the room as quietly as she had entered it.

Bill swore long and emphatically. He'd handled the whole interview in the stupidest possible way. But then it was all so unexpected. He hadn't had time to think. What he should have done was to refuse her right away — tell her to go to Brisbane with whatever nasty little story she chose to tell and that he and Noni would deny it, insist on their innocence.

'*But we aren't innocent!*' Bill spoke the words aloud. The very fact that he'd felt guilty had betrayed him in his handling of Sarah. He hadn't handled her — she handled him — and very efficiently, right down to the last parting shot — 'Discuss it with Mrs Brisbane'. Yes, Sarah had known he'd want to do that. Just as she knew what Noni's answer would be. Noni would do anything to protect Philip. He could very easily afford the hundred pounds. Noni could probably find as much if he were unable to. There was nothing to discuss unless Noni could be made to see the dangers of giving in to blackmail.

He was still stunned with surprise that Sarah, of all people, could have stooped to this. And yet, on reflection, it was not so odd. She did have these strange burning obsessions. She had a grudge against men, too, due to her unhappy experience with the man she'd loved as a girl. When he first knew her he'd thought that she was the type who would have made an excellent suffragette. Sarah was, in fact, a South African, but she had lost both her parents early in life and had been brought up by an aunt she did not like. As soon as she could, she had left home to come to England and had never had any desire to go back.

She was self-sufficient, independent and inclined to be a lone wolf, making few friends with the other nurses. She was an efficient nurse and a good companion and despite everything, Bill liked her. Even now, he had no doubt that this rather nasty thing she was doing to him was not for her benefit but for an 'ideal' or an 'idea'.

He wondered whether he should tell Noni. It wouldn't serve any useful purpose except to worry her and he decided against it. If Sarah was going to nurse Brisbane, she and

Noni were bound to see quite a bit of each other. The more natural Noni could be in her presence the better. He must get an assurance from Sarah that nothing would make her say one word which would lead Brisbane to suspect Noni.

For the hundredth time, Bill wished everything could be out in the open; that he could go himself to Brisbane and tell him the truth. He remembered that Noni was seeing Herod this morning and had promised to phone him. Now it was lunch time and he'd heard nothing. Maybe this second appointment had been put off. He'd have to try to get through a busy afternoon somehow and then, if Noni hadn't phoned, ring her when he got off duty.

He sighed deeply, suddenly desperately tired and anxious. If he hadn't been so deeply in love with Noni, he'd have backed out of the whole set-up long ago. Taking another man's wife was not in his private moral code. He'd always steered clear of married women. He'd seen far too many tormented and unhappy people in his work made so because of adulterous entanglements; jealousy or guilt — both played havoc with the human emotions and through them, the brain. But like so many of his own patients, Bill felt that his case was different. Philip Brisbane had never given anything worthwhile to his marriage; had never tried to win the love and companionship of his wife. He was an emotionally immature type of man who should never have married at all — far less to a sensitive, highly emotional woman like Noni.

But the fact that he knew for a certainty that he could make Noni happy, was no consolation — indeed, it was almost the opposite since it looked so unlikely that he would ever be given the chance to do so.

6

'So you're leaving us tomorrow, Mr Brisbane!'

From his chair by the window, Philip turned his head toward the sound of Sarah's voice and said:

'Yes, thank God. Though only for a couple of weeks. Then I go to Bradstone Hospital for the operation.'

Sarah was silent. The quarrel between Philip Brisbane and the Ophthalmic surgeon, Mr Herod, was common knowledge in the hospital. Philip had removed himself from Herod's care and the operation was going to be performed by another man in another hospital.

'I shall miss you, Sarah!'

She was making his bed and she paused, momentarily taken by surprise at the compliment.

'Thank you! I shall miss you, too.'

'I think you mean that. You know, I wish like hell you were coming home with me. You have a way of cheering me up, giving me back my self-confidence. You're good for me, Sarah.'

'*In a way that your wife isn't!*' Sarah

thought. Philip was always at his worst after one of Noni's visits — irritable and impatient and demanding. It could take her ten minutes of extreme tact to joke him out of the mood.

'I've got something for you, Sarah. Come over here!'

He put his hand in his dressing-gown pocket and drew out a long thin box. Sarah opened it and, losing her accustomed self-control, gasped. It was a tiny diamond wrist watch, beautifully made and unmistakably very expensive.

'I don't think I ought to accept this, Mr Brisbane,' Sarah said haltingly. But Philip laughed.

'Nonsense, you've earned it, and don't call me Mr Brisbane.'

Sarah thoughtfully relaxed. She slipped the watch into her pocket. If Philip Brisbane could afford it, why should she refuse? There was no unbreakable rule about accepting gifts from grateful patients. Presumably Noni must know about it; probably she had been the one to buy it. Sarah wondered what Noni had thought of Philip's extravagance. The watch couldn't have cost much less than a thousand pounds.

'Er, Sarah? Don't mention this to my wife. I don't think she fully appreciates how much you have done for me. I . . . I think it would be best kept as a little secret between us, eh.'

'Very well!'

'You're not shocked? No, of course, you're a sensible girl. Got a practical outlook — a good head on your shoulders. Tell me, Sarah, what do *you* want out of life?'

'The same as any other woman — a home, security, money!'

Philip laughed.

'In that order, I wonder? I find this interesting. So you're not dedicated to your profession? Nursing to you isn't a vocation?'

'I'd leave here tomorrow if I had something better to go to!'

'You would, eh? Well, how about becoming my private nurse?'

For a moment, Sarah felt her heart jolt with pleasure. Then she said quietly:

'But if the operation is a success, you won't need a nurse.'

He did not, as she had expected, reply at once. When he did so, his voice was several tones lower.

'Strictly between us, Sarah, I'm not really very hopeful. I don't like Herod but I have to admit the man knows his job backwards. If he says I'll never be able to see properly again, then I don't think there is much hope.'

'Oh, nonsense!' Sarah said sharply, her professional training coming to the fore. 'You told me only yesterday that the new man, Seagrave, has been in America and has some new techniques.'

Philip sighed.

'Well, we'll see. I'm not expecting any miracles. But if the worst comes to the worst, Sarah, would you leave hospital life and come as my private nurse? I could probably offer you a much better salary and all home comforts. I have a nice house — you should come out and visit us sometime and see it. Come on your next half day — Noni wouldn't mind. Why not do that, Sarah, and then you'll have had time to think over my offer.'

'Then you are serious?'

'Absolutely! I like you, Sarah, and I think you like me?'

'Yes, of course I do!'

'And you really like the watch? I got my night nurse to write to Cartier for me. I think she thought it was for my wife! I'll have to get her something, too, of course, but that can wait. I wanted you to have this before I left.'

'It's extremely generous of you. I'm quite overcome. I don't know how to tell you how pleased I am. I've never had such a magnificent present from anyone in my whole life!'

Her remarks, sincere enough, pleased

Philip. He didn't regret his generosity. It might pay dividends if things came to the worst and he wanted a private nurse. And he could afford to have one if he wished. He and Noni had not spent a great deal of money in their married life, except on their home; and he had put away a good bit, invested wisely on the stock market. With what he'd put by and with the amount of compensation he was pretty certain to get, he wasn't going to be at all badly off even if he never worked again.

His mind swerved away from the thought. The possibility was all too likely and he was not willing to accept that his career had come to an end. Somehow he was going to operate again — *he had to be able to operate again.* His work was his life — he'd give up everything else but not that . . .

'Your bed's ready when you feel like getting back into it,' Sarah said, coming to stand beside his chair. 'But I expect you prefer to sit up for a while. I'm sorry I haven't time to stay and read the papers to you.'

'That's all right — Noni should be here any minute. How do you get on with my wife, Sarah? Think you two might be friends?'

Privately Sarah doubted it. Noni and she were far too different in type ever to become intimate friends. However, she said:

'I think she seems a very sweet person!'

'Wouldn't have made a good nurse, though,' Philip joked. 'Far too soft-hearted.' He broke off as he heard the door open and Sarah say warningly:

'Good morning, Mrs Brisbane!'

'Good morning, Sister. Hullo, Philip!'

Feeling self-conscious with Sarah's eyes on her, Noni walked across to Philip's chair and touched his cheek with her lips. After the cold air outside, his skin felt warm. He was newly shaved and had the now familiar hospital smell of antiseptic about him.

Sarah went out, leaving them alone. Noni pulled up a chair and sat down opposite Philip.

'I've brought the papers and your mail!' she said. 'I think you'll want to dictate a reply to your solicitor. There's a letter from your father, too, and . . .'

'Never mind all that for a moment, I want to discuss something else with you. I've been thinking about the future, Noni, and I've just been having a word with Sarah — Sister Bristow.' He paused, unaware of the hot wave of colour which rushed into Noni's cheeks. What had Sarah been telling him? If she had mentioned Bill . . . 'I thought it might be a good idea, if the operation isn't a success, for her to come and live with us — be a kind of nurse-companion.'

For a moment she was too confused to reply. First was relief that Sarah had not been gossiping to Philip. Then surprise that Philip could actually admit that the operation might not give him back his sight. This was the first time he'd voiced such a possibility. Then the further surprise that he could be contemplating employing Sarah Bristow in a private capacity.

'Well, are you for or against the idea in principle?'

'But Philip, I don't see why you should need a nurse. I'll be there to do things for you.'

'Yes, I know, but you're not exactly a trained nurse, are you?' Philip's voice now held the familiar note of irritation. 'This girl's very efficient and anyway, there'll be plenty for you to do without having to cope with things like shaving me, for example.'

'Won't you be able to do such things for yourself, Philip? I believe the training for blind people is wonderful these days and it's possible to become completely independent, except, of course, for things like driving a car and . . .'

'I don't know why you always have to find objections for any plan I have, Noni. You may be perfectly right about me being able to shave myself — if I want to. But why fumble around in the dark making half a job of it when I can get someone to do it for me professionally?'

She could have argued the point with him but she stayed silent. Philip, in these moods, could be very dogmatic. Arguing or putting a different point of view to his own only aggravated the position.

'Why don't you say something? You do have the most tiresome way of keeping silent. It's really very difficult for me when I can't *see* you. How am I supposed to guess what you're thinking!'

'I'm sorry, Philip. I . . . I was just thinking that it's probably much too soon to be deciding about such things.'

He seemed mollified.

'Yes, you're right, of course. I suppose you haven't talked to Herod again?'

'You asked me not to do so. You said you'd prefer I never spoke to the man again. Don't you remember?'

'All right, I was only asking. I thought you might have bumped into him. What about Aden? Have you been to see him yet.'

'Philip, I don't want to see a psychiatrist. There is nothing wrong with me and it would be a waste of everyone's time and money. Please don't let's discuss that again.'

'Have it your own way. I'll be home

tomorrow, you know. First chance we'll have had for ages to be alone. I hope you'll be in the mood, Noni.'

She caught her lower lip between her teeth. She knew very well what her husband was talking about. If they had been a normal married couple, she might have been as anxious as he was to be alone with him after all these weeks. Now his words sounded like a threat and she wasn't sure if she could go through with what had become a mental ordeal. Maybe Bill was right and she ought to have told Philip the truth. If he knew she was in love with another man, he wouldn't want to make love to her . . . Another long silence. 'You're not exactly what one could call stimulating company, are you, my dear?'

'Philip, please stop criticizing me. That's the third critical remark you've made since I came in!'

'Okay, calm down!' Philip seemed more amused by her brief retaliation than annoyed by it. 'I know what's eating you — you're jealous of my red-head. Why don't you admit it?'

She rose quickly and went across to the window, her back towards him. Nearly every moment of these hours with Philip were a form of torture. She could never be herself; each remark he made began to seem like a deliberate probe in the sore place of her guilt. If only Philip could realize that she no longer *cared*. The only jealousy she had ever felt for Sarah Bristow was because she had once been Bill's mistress. That jealousy would have been manifest if *Bill* had called her 'my red-head'.

As if he could read her thoughts, Philip said:

'I was having a talk with the night nurse about her. I was right, you know, Noni. Sarah did have an affair with Aden. He's not married, of course, and all the girls began to wonder if Sarah was going to produce an engagement ring. But nothing happened. Curious fellow, Aden. Not my type, of course, but I can see why women find him attractive. As a psychiatrist, he must understand the peculiar workings of the female mind. I'll bet he had some fun psychoanalysing Sarah!'

His chuckle offended her almost more than his words. She burst out:

'I don't think there is anything between them now.'

'Oh, really? He's got himself another woman, I expect. Oh, well, we can't waste the morning gossiping. Let's hear what's in the mail.'

Somehow the morning dragged past. Sarah came in with coffee and went out again almost at once. Mr Harvey came in and insisted Noni remain while he talked to Philip.

'I'm sorry you're leaving us like this, Brisbane. I had a long talk with Herod and he assured me it must have been a misunderstanding on your part. I have to say I agree. He really isn't the kind of man to make irresponsible remarks on such a grave matter. Are you still quite adamant that you won't clear things up between you before you go?'

'Nothing to clear up!' Philip said, his mouth tight. 'I don't hold it against Herod, but I'm not going back on my plan to let Seagrave operate.'

'No, of course not. I wish you the very best — we all do. We'll all be hoping like hell that you'll be back in the operating theatre before the end of the year.'

'I'll be back!' Philip said grimly. 'Like to bet?'

Harvey gave an uneasy smile which only Noni saw.

'I never bet on such issues, but whatever happens, if there's anything I can do at any time . . . '

'Yes, thanks!'

'There is just one other thing. You might like to know the form if . . . well if things *don't* go the way we hope. Seagrave would have to fill in a form so that you can be put on the Register of the . . . er . . . Blind. Then the local authority would send one of their visitors to call on you at home — explain things to you — start you on Braille and that kind of thing. In the ordinary way, Herod as Ophthalmic Surgeon of this hospital in charge of your case would be doing this, but as you're taking yourself out of his hands, it'll be up to Seagrave. Just thought I should mention it.'

He shook hands with Philip and, with a smile to Noni, left the room. Noni noticed that Philip's hands were shaking and only then guessed what Harvey's words had done to him. For the first time, he was really having to face up to the fact that he might well remain blind; be registered as blind; have to learn a blind man's alphabet, Braille . . . Pity for him surged through her so violently she could not restrain the hand that went out to cover his.

For a moment he let it remain there. Then he said roughly:

'What's all this about? I hope you aren't being *sympathetic* again, Noni.'

She withdrew her hand quickly, her cheeks burning.

'It's nearly lunch time,' she said. 'I told Mrs Reeves I'd be home for lunch. I'll see you this afternoon if that's okay?'

He was still sitting, a little hunched, in his chair by the window as she opened the door and turned to look at him. The desire to escape became an even greater desire to stay with him; to run to him and put her arms round him and say: 'Don't mind so much, Philip. Don't let it get you down. I'm here. I'll help you. I want to help you!'

But he didn't want her pity any more than he wanted her love. There was nothing she could do for him — nothing anyone could do for him unless it was this man, Seagrave, giving him back his sight.

★ ★ ★

As she closed the door softly behind her, she became aware of voices from the adjoining room — Sarah's voice and Bill's. Sarah's door was open and Noni could not pass it without being seen. She stayed where she was, hesitating, and their next words reached her clearly:

'There's only fifty pounds here, Sarah. I'll get the rest tomorrow.'

'That's okay, Bill. There's no frantic hurry, as long as it's this week.'

'I still don't like it, Sarah. The more I think about it, the more wrong I feel it is. There must be an easier way out.'

Noni knew that she should move away. Whatever they were discussing, it was obviously not meant for her ears, but she could not take that first step. Curiosity had her in its grip. Why was Bill giving Sarah money? And what was he helping to do which he felt was wrong? She had to know.

'. . . other way, you tell me what it is. Take my word for it, Matron would find out somehow if one of *her* nurses was having a baby. And Matron has some pretty old-fashioned morals. Frankly, I'm scared stiff of her myself!'

'How many months, Sarah?'

'She is over the legal limit. So you see, there isn't all that much time.'

Bill's voice was charged with uneasiness.

'You seem so sure this is the right thing to do. I wish I felt so sure. After all, I'm part of it — responsible for what happens.'

'You're not going back on your promise, Bill? You said you'd help me.'

'I don't seem to have much choice, do I, Sarah? I'm in your hands. But that doesn't relieve me of responsibility.'

Noni was suddenly aware that she was shivering. She wanted to cover her ears now, to un-hear that terrible self-indictment of Bill's. All she could think of was that Sarah's unwanted baby had been conceived several months ago. That meant Sarah was still Bill's mistress when he first made love to *her*...

She felt violently sick. A chair scraped the floor in Sarah's room and Noni slipped quickly against the wall. When Bill pushed the door fully open to come out, she was hidden from his view. She could not see him walking away from her down the corridor. But she could hear his footsteps and as they drew further and further away, she realized that he was walking out of her life. No matter what happened to Philip, she would never be able to marry Bill now. She had believed him without question when he'd sworn to her that Sarah was a part of his past — that their affair was over long ago. Now she reminded herself bitterly that he must still have been Sarah's lover when he took *her* away for that first weekend.

Mercifully, Sarah did not leave her room until after Noni had made her escape. Somehow Noni found her way to the lift and out to the car park. Somehow she drove herself home; told Mrs Reeves she had a tearing headache and could not eat lunch. Then at last, she was alone in her room.

Word by word, she went over the conversation she had overheard. Desperately she sought for some loop-hole, something which could prove Bill's innocence, but there

126

was nothing. Only the terrible incriminating sum of fifty pounds which he was giving Sarah to get rid of their unwanted child.

At least, she told herself bitterly, Bill was facing up to his responsibility in the matter. No wonder he felt badly about it. And what of Sarah! How she must hate Noni for coming into Bill's life at such a moment. However much she might pity herself for her lost illusions, she could still feel some pity for Sarah.

Well, Sarah could have him back. Noni would drop out of Bill's life and he would be free to marry Sarah if he wanted to. It was nothing to do with her ... nothing ... nothing ...

She lay, dry-eyed, her face buried in the pillow. Shame suffused her body. What a silly, idealistic little fool Bill must have thought her with all her romantic talk of 'first' love, theirs being 'a special love'.

'*Bill, Bill!*' she cried silently. '*You, who agreed we would be wrong to cheat Philip, were still cheating me.*'

She tried once more to find excuses for him. He hadn't realized until after that first weekend together that he'd really loved her. Therefore, he hadn't ended his affair with Sarah until afterwards ... '*but so long afterwards!*' she thought helplessly. He must have slept with Sarah after he'd slept with her. It was horrible, horrible. This was the man she had loved.

'*But I still do!*'

The thought was almost as unbearable as the thought of his duplicity. In spite of everything, she still loved him. She never wanted to see him again; never wanted him to touch her again, and yet she would go on loving him, stupidly, against all reason — because she could not help it. She loved him — and hated him. Maybe it was her own fault for putting him on a pedestal. Maybe she had been unfair in investing him with noble qualities he didn't possess. He was just a man, like any man, taking his pleasures where he could. But he'd allowed her to go on thinking that this time everything was different; that this time, unlike the past, he was really in love. Probably he would say the same to the next woman in his life. Probably that was what he had once said to Sarah . . .

Mrs Reeves knocked and opened the door.

'Mrs Brisbane, I'm dreadfully sorry to disturb you, but it's the hospital. You're wanted on the phone. Shall I plug it in here for you? It's urgent, or I wouldn't have disturbed you.'

7

She would never have taken the call if she had known it was Bill. Stupidly, she imagined an urgent telephone message from the hospital must be from or about Philip.

'Noni? It's Bill. I hoped I'd catch you at home at lunch time. Darling, I have to see you this evening. It's urgent . . . and important.'

The sound of his voice was a mixture of agony and pleasure.

'I can't see you, Bill.'

Somehow she forced the words out. It was not going to be so easy to resist the sheer magnetism his voice held for her. She had to be strong now. It *must* be all over between them.

'Darling, are you all right? Your house-keeper said you were in your room. You're not ill, are you? Noni, for heaven's sake answer me.'

He still sounded the same Bill — very much in love and full of tenderness and concern for her welfare. She must keep remembering that this was just Bill — the way he was with all women he got involved with. It was part of the charm he could lay on at will.

'Noni? Are you there? Please answer me, darling!'

With great effort, she said:

'I can't see you this evening or any other evening. It's all finished, Bill. I don't ever want to see you again.'

'Noni! What's happened? I just don't understand what all this is about. Has something happened to Philip? For God's sake, darling, don't just come out with brutal statements like that one without explanation. What's wrong?'

Her hands gripped the receiver so tightly that her knuckles shone white through the skin. There was little point in prolonging this conversation. It *had* to come to an end and the sooner the better. She would give him his explanation.

'Bill, I was in the corridor outside Sister Bristow's room when you were with her. I know you gave her some money and I know what it was for. Now do you understand?'

'No, I don't. As a matter of fact, that's what I wanted to talk to you about. If you were there, why on earth didn't you come in?'

He sounded so unperturbed that she was momentarily confused.

'It was a private conversation — I couldn't

very well barge in on you, could I? I didn't mean to eavesdrop but ... well, I just couldn't help hearing.'

'I can understand you disapproving, Noni, but what I don't understand is why you're refusing to see me. I don't see how it affects *us*. I just don't understand.'

'Oh, Bill!' Her voice was a cry of anguish, a plea to him to try to see this from her point of view. 'Maybe it doesn't seem so awful to you ... perhaps Philip is right and I am a prude. But I think *any* woman would feel as I do.'

'All right, Noni, so you don't approve. Nor, in fact do I and I told Sarah so. But I still don't see why I'm so frightful you can't see me any more. It just doesn't make sense.'

'You admitted your responsibility.'

'I don't deny it. If I give Sarah money, then I'm condoning the whole beastly business. But what else could I do, Noni? It's for your sake and mine, that I've agreed to help her.'

'For *my* sake?'

'Well, Sarah could tell Philip. I don't say she would, but she might. You're the one who's dead against him knowing about us. As far as I am concerned, I'm willing to confess the lot. I don't know if I'm strong enough to go on like this. God damn it, I *love you*, Noni.'

She realized for the first time that somehow

or other they were talking at cross purposes. Philip didn't come into this. She felt her heart racing madly. Her palms were damp. Her head was throbbing.

'Tell me just what you were doing in Sarah's room!'

Bill's voice sounded faintly shocked.

'I thought you knew. What's the matter with you, Noni? You're just not making sense. Are you ill? I'm coming over to see you. Something's wrong and I've got to know what it is.'

'No! I don't want you here in this house.'

'Noni! What do you think I'm made of — stone? I'll go crazy if you go on like this much longer. I'm *going* to see you. Whatever it is, we're going to straighten it all out.'

'I don't think it can be straightened out.'

'Of course it can. Am I coming to see you or will you come and see me? It's going to be one or the other, Noni.'

She knew he meant it. She said:

'I'll come to your room at the hospital. What time will you be free?'

'Hold on . . . ' She could hear him moving things on his desk; could visualize the hands she had loved so much touching the books and papers on his table . . . 'My last appointment is at three. I should be through by three-thirty. Promise me you will come?

You won't back out, no matter what's wrong? I just don't trust you in your present frame of mind. *Promise* me, Noni?'

She gave him her promise and rang off. Nothing seemed to make sense any more. Bill hadn't sounded in the least worried that she'd overheard his conversation with Sarah. Perhaps he thought she could take it in her stride that Sarah was carrying his child; that he was helping her to get rid of it! If so, he didn't really know her at all.

Mrs Reeves came in again with some hot soup. She stayed until Noni had finished it.

'You know, Mrs Brisbane dear, you're going to be ill if you go on like this. You must keep your strength up. With Mr Brisbane home tomorrow, you'll be needing every ounce of strength. Now, why don't you stay there this afternoon and have a nice nap?'

'I can't, Mrs Reeves. I've got to go back to the hospital. I've promised my husband . . . and then I've an appointment with one of the doctors at half-past three.'

'There, then that's a good thing. It's high time you had a check-up. I was only saying to Doris last week that you were looking very poorly. You don't look after yourself. And maybe I shouldn't be saying this, but Mr Brisbane doesn't look after you as he should either. But then he's probably so used to seeing really sick people, he doesn't notice if a body is just ailing. You need someone to take care of you, Mrs Brisbane, and that's a fact.'

The kindly sympathy was almost too much for Noni. She struggled against the desire to weep; to be able to unload all that was on her mind. She wanted to be able to cry out:

'I'm not unwell — just unhappy. I'm not in love with my husband. I'm hopelessly in love with another man. Now I'm not even sure if he's worth loving and even if he is, I can't marry him because Philip is blind . . . '

Instead she said quietly:

'Please don't worry about me, Mrs Reeves. I'm just tired. I expect I need a tonic or something.'

Alone once more she got up and changed her clothes and with exaggerated care, re-made up her face and did her hair. This, she told herself hysterically, would probably be the last time she would ever see Bill. It was important that she should look nice.

★ ★ ★

Bill waited for the nurse to bring in the first of the afternoon's patients. This was a young man from the psychiatric ward who had been under his care for six months and was at last beginning to show signs of recovery. He'd come to Bill believing, with all the force of his sick mind, that his uncle was trying to kill him. The boy was over the worst — could even laugh now about the absurdity of the thought that his favourite uncle was trying to poison him. All the same, he had not yet reached the point where he was willing to face his uncle.

'It's not that I don't want to see him — I do!' he said, earnestly to Bill as the interview began. 'It's just that . . . that . . . '

'Now, come on, Robert, say it.'

The boy gave a shy smile.

'It sounds so crazy. You might think I'm going out of my mind again!'

Bill smiled back at him.

'If you knew some of the really crazy things I hear in this room, you'd know that nothing you could say will surprise or alter my opinion of you. I *know* you are better. I know you aren't, as you put it, going out of your mind again. Once you know that what you are going to say sounds crazy, then you can be certain you aren't crazy.'

'Yes, that's right!' the boy agreed. 'When you're sick it's the crazy things that seem real, isn't it!'

'So! And now tell me why you don't want to see your uncle just yet!'

The boy hesitated but seeing Bill's

expectant face waiting for him to reply, he said slowly:

'Suppose when I see him it triggers off the whole wretched illness all over again?'

Bill relaxed. He'd guessed the boy's reason but he wanted him to face up to his fear by himself.

'It won't! You know that as well as I do, don't you, Robert? You're just anxious to play this two hundred per cent safe. You aren't satisfied with one hundred per cent!' He saw the boy relax, smile. 'We both know it was over-work that caused your mind to give way. Your poor brain became so over-loaded and over-tired that it just couldn't sort out reason from unreason any more. What form that 'unreason' took is purely incidental. You might just as easily have reached the conclusion that you were a Russian spy. Probably if you'd been reading a book about spies at the time of your breakdown, that's the form it would have taken. Instead of that, you were studying poisons and your uncle was helping you because he happens to be a qualified chemist. So you see, Robert, as your brain is now quite well again, the sight of your uncle, even if he arrived holding a large bottle labelled POISON, in his hands, wouldn't trigger off anything but surprise. Your most likely reaction would be: 'What on earth has he brought that into this hospital for. He must be bonkers!' '

The boy laughed. For a few moments, they discussed his immediate future when he was discharged from the hospital.

'No more studying, Robert. You realize that?'

'I guessed as much from what you said last time about the strain of attempting the impossible. I don't even want to become a chemist any more, anyway. What I always wanted to be was a carpenter, but my father was terribly anxious for me to go in for one of the professions and as Uncle was a chemist — well, it just sort of got decided. But I really love carpentry — not big things like houses. I'd like to restore antique furniture. Do you think I could, Mr Aden?'

When the boy had left, Bill found himself wishing that all his cases ended the way Robert's would undoubtedly end — with a square peg in a square hole where it belonged. But his next two patients were far from cured and he knew that one of them at least would have to be referred for surgery. He wondered who would do it now Brisbane was off. His replacement wasn't really a brain expert. They'd have to get a specialist in to do the job. It was a pity about Brisbane.

He realized with a shock that he was

thinking of Noni's husband — not as a man, this time, but as an integral part of the hospital.

Noni — another few minutes and she would be here. What could have been wrong with her? There was nothing new on Brisbane — he'd called Sarah after he'd rung Noni, to find out.

His door opened and the nurse anounced:

'Mrs Brisbane!'

'Thank you, Nurse!'

Noni came in. She looked beautiful — and very ill. As he held back the chair for her, he felt suddenly desperately worried about her. She was so pale that the lipstick made her mouth unnaturally red. The shadows beneath her eyes were enormous. She was somehow managing not to look at him.

He went round the desk and sat down opposite her as if she were one of the patients. She looked so tense and near to breaking point that he felt instinctively the need to treat her like a patient.

'What is it, Noni? Tell me!' he said softly.

'It's . . . it's just that . . . it's all finished between us, Bill.'

She still would not look at him. Very quietly, he said:

'Of course it is if that's the way you want it, Noni. Don't be afraid of me — not of *me*.'

She looked up then, half appealing, half accusing.

'Bill, how . . . *how could you?*'

'You'll have to tell me what it is I've done before I can answer that question.'

'But I don't want to talk about it!'

'Noni, this is ridiculous. I've done something to upset you very badly and you won't tell me what it is. Obviously it has something to do with Sarah. Is it because I gave her the money?'

'Because you had to give her the money!'

'But, Noni, what else would you want me to do? I hate blackmail, too, but I don't think Sarah really meant it to be that way. She just worked out in her mind that I could afford to help and so why not? As Philip's nurse, she could so easily have let something slip . . . however small . . . which would have made him suspicious. I knew how desperately keen you were to keep the truth from him so I thought it best to play safe. If you really feel so strongly about it being blackmail, I'll tell her I've changed my mind.'

'I don't see what Philip has to do with it. If Sarah's having a baby, it's surely no concern of his.'

'Sarah having . . . Noni, darling, Sarah *isn't* having a baby. It's one of the young nurses in . . . *Noni!*' Suddenly he knew what she had been thinking and he became furiously angry. 'You thought Sarah was having *my* child. My God, you didn't trust me very much, did you? I told you Sarah and I had our bust-up six months ago. I thought you believed me.'

'I did, Bill, I did! Until this morning when I heard you up there ... Oh Bill please darling if it isn't true, I'm sorry!'

'And so you damn well ought to be!' He caught sight of her stricken face and all anger left him as he was hit by a wave of love for her. He got up and went over to her and lifted her up into his arms and rocked her back and forth like a child. He could feel her tears salt beneath his lips.

'Darling, darling, my silly, *silly* darling! No wonder you were talking so crazily about 'never seeing me again'. You thought that Sarah and I ... Noni, my darling, silly little love ... can't you understand that from the moment I first held you in my arms when we danced together, no other woman has had the slightest interest for me. Kim Basinger could walk in here stark naked and I wouldn't be interested. I'm in love with *you*. You may not be all that beautiful or have so much sex appeal or whatever, but you're everything, *everything* I want.'

Noni wept quietly and openly. She no longer cared if anyone came in and saw her.

She didn't care about anything but that Bill loved her, had always loved her and that she had somehow been fool enough to imagine quite unfair and unworthy things about him.

'Forgive me, forgive me!' she cried, clinging to him fiercely as if he might turn away from her in disgust and leave her.

'Darling, sssh! In a way, it's partly my fault. I should have told you when Sarah first approached me for money. Then today, after I'd given her half what she'd asked for, I was suddenly terribly afraid I was doing something very wrong — or helping to do it. I thought I should ask you whether you felt I should go ahead or if we could risk her talking to Philip. That's why I phoned you. In a way, you were already involved though you didn't actually know what was going on. It came to me that you had a right to know.'

'Sarah's going to help some girl get rid of her baby?'

'Yes! It's one of the younger nurses. Sarah wants to send her to a private clinic where it can be done quickly.'

'And you don't think we should be part of it?'

Bill released her and walked over to the window.

'I suppose it sounds a bit silly, coming from me, but the fact is, I don't approve of a woman deliberately ending the life of an embryo which could survive at that stage. It ought to be possible for a girl to have her child and keep it if she wants to. I know things are much better than they used to be, but they still aren't right. It's back to my old bug-bear, Noni — fear. This girl is afraid and so she wants to kill her unborn child. I doubt if she'd want to kill it if she wasn't afraid.'

'Then if you feel like that, we won't help,' Noni said softly. 'I don't like it either. Perhaps we can help the girl some other way?'

'And if Sarah talks to Philip?'

'Then let her. We can deny it. I don't think I mind much any more. Not for myself, anyway. Will Sarah give you the money back?'

'Let me worry about that. Darling, do you realize what it's going to mean to us if we do have to stop seeing each other? I don't think it's going to be possible. How can I stay away from you knowing that you are miserable and lonely? And you, Noni, how will you manage your life with Philip now?'

'Don't, Bill. I don't want to think about it!' She shivered in his arms.

'My darling, you've got to think about it. I ran into Herod — or rather he sent for me — not about Philip, of course; we're 'liaising' over a brain tumour; but before I left him *he* mentioned Philip to me; asked me if I'd heard what had been going on. Then he told me. Noni, he's absolutely certain — without one shadow of a doubt — that Philip will never be able to see properly again. There is not an iota of a chance that he can ever operate again. It's just a question of whether some tiny particle of vision can be restored — enough for Philip to see vague objects. Herod thought the case might interest me because he's convinced Philip deliberately misinterpreted his verdict because he wasn't mentally prepared to accept the truth. A classic case of 'wishful thinking'. But Philip will have to accept it eventually — from this other man, Seagrave. It's a fact, Noni. So you see, we've got to decide what we are going to do.'

In one way, she was neither shocked nor surprised. She'd been prepared for the worst. But she had steadfastly refused to consider what her life would be like without Bill. *Was* she strong enough? It would take a very strong woman indeed to give up everything for a man she didn't love and who didn't love her.

'But I can't hurt Philip — not now!' She spoke her thoughts aloud.

Bill's grip on her arms tightened.

'I have to say this, even if you hate me for it, Noni — but *will he be so very hurt?* He

143

doesn't love you — not the way you and I understand the meaning of love. His pride will suffer, but will he? I know in theory this idea of self-sacrifice is very noble and praiseworthy, but will it work out in practice? Does any marriage work where the two parties have ceased to love one another? Ought we to let Philip's accident affect the decision we reached before pity clouded the issue?'

'It was different before!' Noni whispered. 'He had his work and it meant everything in the world to him. I don't think he would have minded my leaving. His work was always so much more important to him than I was. But now . . . can't you see, Bill . . . now he'll have nothing. I *have* to stay with him.'

'And if your doing so fails to make him happy?'

'Then I suppose there would be no point in my staying with him. But I have to try, Bill — for a while, anyway. Philip comes home tomorrow. I mustn't see you, talk to you — even think about you if I can help it. I want to do my best and I can't if all the time I'm remembering *you*.'

Bill's face was miserable. This might be the last time he would ever hold her in his arms. He wanted to argue with her, make her see that it would never work, that she couldn't walk out of his life like this. Yet he had to respect her point of view. She might be the woman he loved but, primarily, she was Mrs Philip Brisbane and no matter what it cost them both, she wasn't going to walk out on her obligations. Nor had he the right to try to make her.

'Bill, I'm so sorry! Please don't be so unhappy. I'll go on loving you all my life. I can't help it. Even when I thought that you and Sarah . . . I still couldn't stop loving you. I'm glad I was wrong about you both. Now I'll only be able to remember good things. I'm not sorry about anything . . . I don't regret a single moment we've shared. Even if meeting you and loving you has to end with this . . . this kind of heartbreak, I'm still glad we met and knew each other. Say you are too, Bill. Say you aren't sorry we fell in love!'

'Noni!' He couldn't answer her. All he could think of was that at any moment now, she would walk out of this room, out of his life. It would have been so much easier if he'd thought she would be happy; if Brisbane really loved her and would be good to her. But her husband was more likely to become irritable, difficult, aggressive, once he realized his career was at an end. He might even take it out on Noni — someone upon whom he could vent his anger and frustration. And she looked so pale and tired and ill. She needed someone to look after her — to cherish *her*.

He kissed her with a kind of violent desperation. He could feel her body trembling and wondered if she was crying. He wished he could cry. It took all his self-control not to fight her decision. He had to remember that he was letting her go for *her* sake and not for Philip's — for *her* peace of mind.

She drew away from him, touched his cheek once very briefly with her finger tips, and then ran out of the room.

He stood staring after her, unable to believe that she had really gone, and yet knowing from the aching pain around his heart that it was all over.

8

'What's the matter, Bill? Aren't you well?'

Sarah looked at the man's drawn face with professional concern. He certainly didn't look well. Or maybe he was just tired at the end of a long day. There'd been a time when he'd come off duty too exhausted to do anything much but sleep.

'I'm okay! I came up to see you, Sarah, because I want that money back.' His voice was toneless, almost automatic. 'I've changed my mind.'

Sarah's eyebrows went up slightly.

'Oh? I wonder why.'

'That's really not your business. Are you going to give it back?'

She reached into the drawer of the table and drew out the roll of notes he'd given her earlier that day, and handed them to him, enjoying the faint look of surprise that crossed his face.

'As a matter of fact, I was going to give it back anyway. It's not needed any more. Apparently the boy-friend is going to marry the girl after all.'

Bill let out his breath.

147

'That's okay, then. But while we're on the subject, Sarah, I'll offer some advice — keep out of other people's troubles. I'm sure you really wanted to help this girl but it's a dangerous business to try and arrange other people's lives for them, even if you are doing it for the best.'

Sarah sat down and lit a cigarette.

'Perhaps you'd benefit from the same advice?' she said pointedly. Bill took a step forward — his face darkening. Irrelevantly, Sarah thought how attractive he looked when he was angry. He was attractive . . . it wasn't so easy to forget how much she'd once wanted him; and always there'd been that wanting more from him than he'd been prepared to give.

'Would you mind explaining what you're talking about?'

She gave a genuine laugh of amusement.

'Don't go all pompous, Bill — at least, not with me. You know damn well what I'm referring to. What's the point in our talking in riddles? I know you and Noni Brisbane are in love. I expect you've been sleeping with her, too.'

'Since you know so much,' he said furiously, 'then you might as well know that it's all over. We're not seeing each other any more.'

'So the good little wife is going to do the 'Right Thing' and go back to her 'Poor Injured Better Half!''

'My God, Sarah, do you have to belittle everything?'

'I think perhaps I do. There isn't room in this tough little world of ours for sentimentality. Life's hard, Bill, and a girl has to learn some way how to take the knocks.'

Some of the anger left him. He looked down at Sarah more kindly. Life *had* been tough with her and in a way, she was right. If one was too sentimental, one got hurt. He was hurt. He could understand her attitude.

Sarah watched Bill, her eyes thoughtful. She, too, had heard the rumours about Philip Brisbane. And the hospital grapevine had a way of being right. The nurses had been discussing it at lunch. There was no hope of a cure for him. The man was blind and would stay so.

For a moment, Sarah had felt her heart leap at the news. She remembered Philip's wish to have her as his private nurse and already she had made up her mind she would take the job if it was offered to her. Philip liked her and she'd already felt a measure of his generosity! But then one of the other nurses said:

'I expect he'll go to that rehabilitation

centre at Torquay. That's where they sent my aunt. She learned how to look after herself there and they taught her Braille and then she went to train as a masseuse. Now she's completely independent.'

So she wasn't going to be needed after all! Back to the dreary round of ward nursing and nothing, *nothing* to look forward to. Only the occasional hospital dance . . .

'What are you doing this evening, Bill?' she asked suddenly.

'I'm going to get very quickly and very completely drunk!'

She gave a deep husky laugh.

'No, that'll only lead to a hangover. There's a dance on tonight, Bill. Take me . . . '

'I couldn't possibly . . . ' he began, but broke off. Why not! What did it matter what he did so long as it helped him to stop thinking about Noni. Anything would be better than the haunting memory of Noni's unhappy little face as she walked out of his room. One thing he must avoid was being alone. He'd be tempted to telephone her; tempted to beg her to see him . . .

'All right, I'll take you!' he said.

'I'm off duty in ten minutes!' Sarah told him, the quietness of her voice belying her inner excitement. 'Give me an hour to bath and change.'

'I'll meet you in the Chequers at seven!' Bill said. 'We might as well have a few drinks and something to eat first.'

'I'll be there!' Sarah promised.

Immediately after he left her, Bill regretted the momentary weakness which had prompted him to tell Sarah he would take her to the dance. He had no wish for her company — or for anyone else's. But, equally, he could not be bothered to go back and tell Sarah he'd changed his mind. Maybe, in any event, it was the best thing to do. He didn't want to antagonize her — give her any reason for telling Brisbane.

He had a wash and went out of the hospital and down the road to the Chequers. It was more a roadhouse than a pub and a great many of the hospital staff used it as a kind of club room. Bill avoided tables at which were people he knew and sat on a bar stool between two complete strangers who did not try to draw him into conversation. He had a double brandy and felt a bit better. He had another and knew that he was beginning to get a little drunk. In this state, the thought of Noni was just bearable. He toyed with the idea of going into the telephone booth and talking to her but had sufficient self-will left not to do so. He had another brandy instead.

When Sarah joined him, he was good-humouredly tight.

''lo, Pretty Woman,' he greeted her. 'Have a drink!'

Sarah eyed him speculatively.

'What you need is food!' she said. But she sat down on the now vacant stool beside him and let him order two more drinks.

'Damn lonely here till you came!' Bill mumbled. 'Feeling pretty down in the dumps. You sheer me up, Sharah!'

He put a hand on her arm and although the gesture was meant more as a support for himself than as any kind of desire for a flirtation, Sarah felt the nerves beneath her bare skin jolt. Bill had always been able to do this to her whether he meant to or not. There was the familiar ache of desire and a simultaneous sharpening of her mind as she recognized and admitted it.

'Poor old Bill!' she said gently. 'Lost your girl-friend!'

'Trying to forget it!' Bill corrected her. 'Thash the only thing to do — forget!'

'I'll help you to forget her, Bill. We always had fun together, didn't we? We'll have fun this evening.'

'Thash right!' Bill said, nodding his head vigorously. Sarah linked her arm in his. When the barman stopped in front of them, she ordered sandwiches. She couldn't take Bill to the dance if he were too tight. He must sober up a bit.

At first he refused to eat but eventually she persuaded him. His mood changed and he became noisily gay. One or two of the doctors who knew him came over and joined them. It became quite a party. Bill had his arm round Sarah's shoulders and kept singing: 'Oh, Pretty Woman!' until the bartender hushed him.

At nine o'clock, the party went back to the hospital to the dance. Even in his present state, Bill danced beautifully. Sarah was deliberately provocative, pressing close against him, knowing he had become aware of her body.

'*Noni Brisbane has left him*!' The thought kept hammering through her brain. '*She's left him and if I play my cards right, I might get him back on the rebound.*'

The thoughts in Bill's head were anything but consistent. He was aware of the music, the noise, the heat and the smoke; he was aware of Sarah's body, supple and warm and inviting in his arms. But suddenly he was remembering another dance, another woman in his arms, a woman he loved . . . Noni!

He closed his eyes and held Sarah more tightly. Like this, it was almost possible to believe that it was Noni he held, that Noni was here pressed against his heart.

'Darling, darling!' he whispered, lost in his dreams.

Sarah felt a quick, wild elation. She was still attractive to him, he still wanted her.

'Let's go back to your flat!' she said softly. 'Take me home with you, Bill.'

The dance ended and he stood looking down at her in bewilderment. He'd thought he was with Noni . . . but this was Sarah. She was saying something to him. He ought to listen.

'We could have a drink at your flat, Bill!'

'*That's what I need,*' he thought. '*Another drink.*'

Obediently he allowed Sarah to guide him through the crowded room. In the corridor it was much cooler and he felt his head whirling. Someone was guiding him along. His legs felt weak and he didn't have the strength to argue about where he was going.

'I'll drive you. You're not fit to!'

He slumped back in the car seat and slept. When he woke a woman was speaking to him. He wasn't sure who she was.

'Bill, here's some coffee. Drink it up. It's nice and hot. I've just made it. *Coffee!*'

Still bemused, he drank the coffee and his head began to clear a little.

'Where's Noni?' he asked stupidly.

Sarah sat down on the settee beside him, curling her stockinged feet beneath her.

'Never mind Noni!' she said. 'You don't need Noni — you've got me, Bill.'

He looked hazily at her as though he did not recognize her. Then he said:

'Oh, it's you, Sarah. Is there any more coffee?'

She gave him another cup. She watched the slackened lines of his face tighten into their usual contour as he began to sober up. She tried to curb her impatience. All evening long she had been longing for the moment when he would make love to her. It had been a long while since the last time and the hunger of her body was becoming painfully insistent. She tried not to think of it as Bill sipped his coffee slowly — maddeningly slowly. To occupy her mind, she looked round the room, seeing it for the first time. Bill had changed his flat since the days when he had taken her home for an hour or two of love. No, not love. Bill had never loved her. But *she* had loved *him*. She *still* loved him. Funny that she should only know that now.

She undid the top buttons of her blouse and saw him staring at her creamy-white breasts. She mistook that stare of incomprehension for one of desire.

'Don't keep me waiting any longer, darling!' she said huskily. 'I want you so much, Bill?'

Impatiently, her hands were tearing at the remaining buttons. She felt Bill's hands covering her own and thought he was trying to assist her. His voice came like a shock of cold water, stunning her into disbelief.

'Sarah, don't! I . . . I can't.'

She looked up then into his eyes. In them she read many things but not desire. There was pity, revulsion, surprise, disbelief — but not desire.

Her cheeks flamed an angry red as the humiliation of her position struck her. Fool, *fool* that she had been! She pulled her blouse across her naked breasts with trembling hands.

'God, Sarah, I'm sorry. I didn't realize . . . you've got to understand . . . I'm three parts tight, Sarah. Surely you understand?'

She understood all too well. Despite his words, Bill was not drunk any more. He was painfully sober. He just did not want her. She'd thrown herself at him and he'd just as surely refused her what she offered him.

'It's Noni, isn't it?' she said viciously. If Noni had come into the room at that moment, she would have killed her. She wanted to kill her.

156

'Get me out of here — take me home!' she shouted at him. 'That is, if you're fit to drive which I doubt.'

'Please, Sarah, don't go like this!'

He was miserably aware of her humiliation. He couldn't begin to think how she had ever imagined he'd wanted to make love to her. But then he'd had so much to drink, heaven alone knew what he might have said to her. Who had suggested they come here to his flat? Had *he* done so? It seemed to him that Sarah had suggested another drink.

She was fully dressed now, her back towards him stiff with pride — or was it anger? He tried once more to get through to her — to make her understand that his rejection of her was not because she wasn't attractive. It was because he couldn't want anyone but Noni . . .

'I love Noni!' he said simply. 'Can't you understand, Sarah? You were in love once — you must remember how it is. Maybe there'll come a time when . . . when I'll be able to forget about her. But it's too soon now. Please, Sarah, try to understand.'

She turned then, her face ugly with the hate of a scorned woman.

'I understand all right. Now call me a taxi.'

In silence, they walked out of the flat when it arrived, Sarah tight-lipped and unbending by his side. Bill would have attempted a last plea for understanding, a last apology, but she slammed the car door behind her and was driven off into the darkness before he could say anything.

He went back to his flat in a state of helpless depression. The last thing in the world he wanted was to hurt the girl. He liked her well enough. *Had* it been his fault? He seemed to be getting into the habit of hurting people. He'd hurt Noni with his love. She'd been, if not happy, at least resigned to her life with Brisbane until he'd come aong. Now he had hurt Sarah.

He'd been crazy getting so drunk he couldn't remember what he'd said and done. He couldn't even remember how he'd got from the dance back to his flat. Presumably Sarah had driven him. *Had* it been his idea? He found it hard to believe. Even in that stupor, he could remember thinking of Noni while he danced.

He felt desperately ill and tired. It was all he could do to walk up the stairs, undress and fall into bed. He ought to have been able to sleep but strangely he could not. Noni's pale little ghost was haunting him, shining out of the darkness, whispering: *'I'll always be glad we loved each other, Bill.'*

158

9

'I thought I told you I didn't want anything moved?'

Philip stood in the doorway of the dining room which, as Noni had just explained, she had turned into a bedroom for him.

'I thought it would be easier for you to be all on one floor; and it would be easier for meals, too!'

He was wearing his warm dressing gown in which he had travelled in the ambulance from the hospital. There were clean white bandages over his eyes. He was frowning.

'Oh well, it's done now. But it's very irritating. I shan't know where anything is.'

Noni took his arm and said eagerly:

'I can soon show you, Philip. Your bed is along the window wall. We put it there so you could reach the telephone. I thought you'd be sure to want to use the phone. Then there's a large table by the bed and an armchair at the foot for visitors. Otherwise the room is empty. I thought . . . ' she hesitated, uncertain of his reaction . . . 'I thought it would be easier if you want to walk about if there wasn't too much furniture to bump into.'

'I suppose I'll manage!' Philip said grudgingly.

He had sent the ambulance away as soon as it reached the front door. He wouldn't allow the men to bring him into the house. The old authority was back in his voice and the men had obeyed him, leaving Noni to assist him.

'I've orders to go straight to bed!' Philip said. 'I suppose I'd better do as I'm told. The old leg isn't as strong as it should be yet.'

Noni helped him into bed. She'd been up late the night before arranging and rearranging things in the room. She wanted Philip to feel really welcomed back. There was a bowl of late roses on the table, especially chosen so he could enjoy the smell. Beside them lay the morning's mail and a pile of medical magazines; a radio with push button-automatic station finding so that he could change the programme with a touch. She began to explain her gift to him. His 'thank you' sounded a little grudging but she tried not to notice it.

He got into bed and lay back against the pillow. She sat down beside him and he said:

'I suppose it's time for the inevitable cup of tea. I think I'll have a sherry instead.'

Noni went out to the kitchen to tell Mrs Reeves to forget the tea-tray.

'Now you'll be feeling a new person, Mrs

Brisbane dear. Having Mr Brisbane home will cheer you up.' Mrs Reeves smiled happily. 'I must say, he looks quite well except for his poor eyes.'

Noni tried not to feel guilty. Having Philip home meant an end to her privacy — an end to so much . . . When she returned with the sherry, Philip said:

'This is a single bed, Noni. Do I take it you prefer to sleep alone.'

As always, the colour flared in her cheeks.

'I . . . I thought it would be best — until you're quite fit again. I mean, we might disturb each other at night, and . . . '

'Noni, I want to talk to you!'

Oh, God, she prayed silently. *Let's not talk about that — not now, not yet.*

'Yes, Philip?'

Was her voice trembling?

'Exactly what is your objection to sleeping with me?'

'Philip, really, this is ridiculous. You're just out of the hospital and I thought . . . '

'Come over here, here beside me!'

He reached out blindly. She could have moved away but she would not take advantage of his blindness. He pulled her roughly into his arms.

'Philip, don't! Mrs Reeves might come in!'

'So what! She can have the pleasure of

watching a wife really welcome her husband home!' He tried to kiss her but she turned her face aside.

'Philip, no! I don't want to.'

He still held her in a vice-like grip but he was no longer trying to kiss her. In a cold angry voice, he said:

'So now we get down to some home truths. You've been carrying on with Mister Bill Aden, haven't you, Noni? Don't deny it, I know all about it. While I was lying in hospital unable to see what was going on under my very nose, you and the hospital Romeo were having a little fun on the sly!'

If he had not been lying there, blind with those bandages over his eyes, she would have hit him.

'It's not true!' she shouted. 'It's not true. We didn't make love once after you had your accident!'

'So you admit you have been unfaithful?'

Then all anger left her. In its place was sorrow and pity for Philip and a relief that at last the truth was known by him.

'Yes, I admit it. I don't know how you found out. I wanted to tell you myself but it didn't seem fair. I fell in love with Bill. I didn't mean to. Neither of us meant it to happen. But it's all over now. I'm never going to see him again.'

'So!' Philip's voice was no longer angry but faintly amused. 'This great romantic love affair has come to an end. The erring wife returns to a forgiving husband. Is that what you are hoping for, my dear?'

'Please, Philip, don't be sarcastic. Of course I want you to forgive me. I'm deeply ashamed of myself . . . ' (even in her desire to save his feelings, she could not say she was sorry about it). 'I give you my word I'll never let it happen again.'

'You know, you interest me, Noni!' His grip on her arms had slackened. His tone of voice had become purely conversational. 'You, the epitome of sexual coldness, were nevertheless tempted to try out the novelty of sex with another man. I would never have thought you were the type to be unfaithful. Quite an interesting state of affairs. As to your choice, you used your head there, didn't you? Why, I suggested myself you should let Aden sort you out. As a matter of interest, did he succeed?'

She tried to keep calm, tried to make allowances for what he must be feeling. It was only natural that, hurt, he would want to hurt her. But there was a limit to how much of this she could take.

'I . . . I'd really rather not talk about it!' she pleaded. 'I want to forget about it. Couldn't we *both* forget it, Philip?'

'Indeed not!' said her husband. 'I'm extremely curious. Maybe this will all turn out to be a blessing in disguise. Maybe now you'll be more interested in sleeping with me!'

She couldn't believe he meant it seriously. This must be an act. No wronged husband could react *this* way. But Philip could. His hands were on her waist, feeling their way upward towards her breasts . . .

'No!' The word burst from her as she tore herself away from his hands. 'Please, Philip, try to understand. If you will give me a little time, then everything can be as it used to be. I promise you; I only need a little time. Just leave me alone for a little while, Philip, *please*.'

'And why the hell should I? You said the affair is all over. Or is that a lie? Maybe you were expecting me to give you a divorce? If so, you've another think coming.'

'No, I don't. I want to stay with you, Philip. I'm never going to see Bill again. But I must have a little time before . . . before I can . . . '

Philip gave a cruel little laugh.

'So Aden didn't succeed in getting you interested in sex. I can sympathize with the poor chap — a hell of a lot of fun he must have gotten out of it. No wonder *he* didn't want to marry you. But I did marry you, Noni, and as your husband, I can demand what he can only ask for.'

She stared at him, horrified.

'Philip, you can't . . . knowing I don't want to.'

'Can't I? Well, I can. That's the funny part about you, Noni. There's something very exciting about you. I'm not quite sure what it is — a sexual challenge, perhaps. You may say you don't want it, but you're asking for it with your voice, your touch, your beautifully soft body. Go and lock the door!'

She was suddenly quite calm. She said:

'I'm sorry, Philip, but I just *can't*!'

Philip's voice was equally calm.

'There's no such word as 'can't', my dear. Besides, if you refuse me, I'll have Bill Aden struck off the register. And I'll see he gets such a lot of stinking publicity that he'll never be able to practice again as long as he lives! Or don't you care what happens to him?'

'You . . . you've no proof, Philip!'

'Haven't I? Do you want to take the gamble, Noni?'

She couldn't be sure. Somehow Philip had found out about her and Bill. With that much knowledge, how could she be certain he didn't have the proof he needed to carry out his threat?

'Well?' said Philip.

She hesitated a moment longer; then she went slowly across the room and locked the door.

★ ★ ★

She made no protest when it was over. Her whole body felt numb. She would be all right provided she did not have to think about it. Philip seemed to have no idea of the violation he had just perpetrated. The fact that she had not fought or resisted him in any way seemed to have restored his good humour. Insensitive as always, he assumed that his wife had come to her senses and was quite happy to fulfil her duty towards him.

He seemed to feel little or no jealousy toward Bill Aden. Or if he did, he made no further reference to him. There were no recriminations about her unfaithfulness; no mention of divorce. He did not appear to be particularly hurt. It was as if he considered that what had just happened had wiped the slate clean. He was better-tempered with her than he had been for weeks.

Throughout the evening meal which Mrs Reeves served them in Philip's room, he kept up an animated conversation for the most part about his impending operation, the effect

166

this might have on the financial compensation which might be awarded him. He told a silent Noni about the new man who had taken over for him at the hospital. In many ways, the evening was like so many hundreds of others before Philip's accident — he talking, she listening. He was not interested in her views and was content to expound his own to his single audience.

Soon after ten he admitted to feeling tired. Noni brought his wash things but he refused her help, preferring to manage as much as he could himself. When she dropped the soap into the basin from sheer nervous exhaustion, he became irritable again:

'You really are hopeless, Noni! The most junior student nurse could manage better.'

She was near to tears when at last he settled down. At least he made no effort to keep her with him. She was free at last to go up to her own bedroom; to the blessed relief of being alone once more.

As she prepared for bed, she kept an iron grip on her thoughts. She would *not* think about this afternoon. If she once let herself remember the selfish and callous manner in which her husband had forced himself upon her, she would not be able to stay with him. She would think about Bill. Another whole day and night had passed and she did not know where he was, what he was doing, if he was happy or as desperate as she was. Tomorrow was Saturday. In the morning she could picture him in his consulting room which she knew so well. But in the afternoon he might be going to play golf, to the races, away for the weekend to stay with friends. She would not know what he was doing . . .

She climbed into bed and put out the light. She was shivering from nervous tension but she knew it would be a long time before she could sleep.

In an effort to forget Bill, she thought about Philip in the room below. She must try to remember that however unhappy and hopeless her life might seem, his must seem to him far worse. She must not hate a man with so much courage. During the whole afternoon and evening, he had not made one complaint about his blindness.

Was it possible, she wondered, that he was becoming adjusted to the idea? Or was he secretly counting on the success of the operation no one but he believed in? Would the seemingly calm acceptance of his fate break when he finally had to give up hope? It would be then he would really need her help. Somehow, she had to be able to give it to him. It was not enough for her just to be his nurse. She must be his companion, too, someone to encourage and support him, to keep him from becoming immersed in depression. It was for this she had given up so much.

For the first time, she had a chance to speculate as to how Philip had discovered the truth. The only possibility seemed to be that Sarah Bristow had told him what she had seen. But Sarah did not know she and Bill were lovers, and Philip had spoken of 'proof' when he had threatened to ruin Bill's reputation. Perhaps Philip was just bluffing. But it made no difference to the outcome. Philip knew and, incredibly, he had taken it almost as a joke . . .

She shuddered. Despite her determination not to think of it, she found herself remembering the way Philip had assumed that she had been experimenting and Bill amusing himself. Seen through Philip's eyes, their love could not have seemed more sordid. She had been too horrified to try and defend something that had been beautiful to her and to Bill, even though it had been morally wrong. Her strong sense of guilt over her act of adultery affected very greatly her behaviour with Philip. She knew that no amount of talking could make the wrong a right, that nothing she could say would make Philip understand what had

169

actually happened between her and Bill. It was outside his conception of things. He didn't believe in love.

Noni was being made to realize very quickly what her future with Philip would be like — the future she had chosen despite Bill's warnings that it could not work. She must make it work. She had to make Philip happy. Maybe it was a good thing Philip knew the truth. Now at least, they could start again and try to build up a new marriage. In time she would learn to overcome this terrible physical revulsion for him and be glad that he still found her attractive. She must try. She must succeed . . .

The clock struck half-past midnight before at last she fell into a troubled sleep.

10

Bill wiped his forehead with his handkerchief and leaned back in his chair. It was nearly lunch time. Mercifully it was Saturday and there would be no more patients this afternoon. He glanced at his appointments book and saw Sarah's note.

'Very important I see you. Will call in at twelve-thirty. V.I.P. S.'

The V.I.P. had once been their private code to denote that there had been a sudden change in plans — something which made a meeting between them really urgent. Despite his wish to get away from the hospital as soon as he could, Bill knew he would have to stay until Sarah turned up. He didn't want to see her. He could remember enough about the night before last to be feeling more than a little embarrassed about the whole unfortunate episode. If it hadn't been for that 'V.I.P.' he wouldn't have waited. Perhaps Sarah had guessed as much. He hoped desperately that she was not going to make a scene, though knowing her, he doubted it. She was more likely to be nursing a large slice of injured pride and be at her most

171

haughty and sarcastic.

The Sarah who came into his office five minutes later was, however, neither of these things. She was unnaturally ill-at-ease and her words came out in a nervous flurry.

'I just had to see you, Bill. I'm so sorry, so very sorry. I know you won't be able to forgive me but I didn't mean to do it, I swear I didn't . . .'

He pushed her gently into the chair used by his patients and handed her a cigarette.

He was frankly very surprised that Sarah could have taken that night's episode in quite this way. It just wasn't like her.

'Calm down, old thing!' he said. 'There's absolutely no reason for you to apologize to me. I'm the one who should be doing that. I was hopelessly tight and . . . well, I just didn't know what I was doing or saying. It's for *you* to forgive *me*, Sarah.'

Suddenly, fantastically, she burst into tears. He had never seen Sarah cry, had thought her all but incapable of tears. This was no weak girl, soft and prone to nervous tensions and emotional upsets. She was far too hardened to life — too stoical for an easy breakdown.

He gave her his handkerchief and waited quietly for her to get herself under control. When she could speak, she said:

'You wouldn't be so nice to me if you knew,

Bill. God, I've been such a bitch!'

She blew her nose and, avoiding his eyes, told him what she had come to say.

'Bill, I told Philip Brisbane about you and Noni!'

'You what?'

At first, he simply did not believe her. No matter what she might have threatened, he'd always believed she would keep her mouth shut. She couldn't have done such a thing . . .

'I told him. I didn't mean to. I was feeling so awful after . . . after the dance. I was hurt and angry and . . . I suppose I might as well admit the lot now . . . I was jealous of Noni Brisbane. She had you *and* Philip Brisbane and it seemed so unfair. Then he started to talk about her . . . I suppose I ought not to have let him . . . he was talking about their private life together and saying how disinterested she was in sex . . . and suddenly I said it — I told him about Noni and you. The moment I'd done it, I wished like hell I hadn't but it was too late. I tried to make him believe I'd just been joking but he's no fool — he knew I wasn't. Bill, I'll do anything I can to put things right . . . *anything at all.*'

'Oh, my God!' Bill stood staring down at her, believing and yet not believing that she could have done this to Noni and him. And

173

for no better reason than sheer vindictiveness. *Hell hath no fury like a woman scorned*! If ever there were a classic example . . .

'I hoped you might be able to think of something I could do to help?'

'Haven't you done enough?'

She bit her lip as the tone of his voice cut across her.

'Do you realize he went home yesterday morning . . . God knows what he'll have said to Noni. For pity's sake, Sarah, what made you do such a rotten thing?'

She didn't cry again but sat twisting his handkerchief between her fingers, her head bent. Despite all she had done, he felt a moment's pity for her. She looked so abject. At least she had had the guts to tell him — that was something in her favour. But this meant the end of their friendship. He'd never be able to like her again.

'Just so you understand exactly what you've been meddling in,' he said bitterly, 'let me enlighten you, Sarah. Noni and I fell in love — *really* in love. We were going to ask Brisbane to divorce Noni so we could get married. Then he had his accident and we decided we couldn't go through with our plans. It wasn't for our sakes we were trying to keep the truth from him. It was for *his* sake. So that's to whom you've done the bad

174

turn, Sarah — not so much to Noni and me.'

'Yes, I know. I lay awake all last night thinking about it. You can't hate me more than I hate myself.'

Bill turned away. He did not want to feel sorry for her. He wanted to be able to focus his thoughts on what could be done now. What had happened to Noni? How had Philip taken it? Was he bullying her? Maybe he'd told her to 'get out' . . .

'I've got to phone her . . . ' he said aloud but Sarah broke in:

'You can't, Bill. I tried, this morning. Philip has the telephone in his room — he's answering all the calls.'

'*You* rang?' Bill echoed.

'Yes! I was going to warn Noni. When I realized I couldn't talk to her, I . . . I decided to come to you.'

'Was Noni at home?'

'I don't know. I had to pretend I was just ringing to find out how *he* was. I was so flustered I didn't think to ask where Noni was. It might have seemed odd.'

'To hell with that. Ring again — make some excuse. Here, do it from my phone. Say you've found some of his belongings in his room and you want Noni to come and fetch them.'

'But I don't think he did leave anything.'

175

'Never mind that. Say the night nurse has made up a parcel of things and you don't know what's in it. I've *got* to see Noni, find out what's happening. You said you'd do anything — well, here's one thing you can do. Ring up, Sarah, *now*!'

He waited impatiently while Sarah reluctantly made the call. It took longer than he'd expected. Philip was in a semi-jocular, semi-flirtatious mood and prolonged the conversation with Sarah. After a moment or two, Sarah said:

'Will Mrs Brisbane be able to come, then?'

Philip's voice was audible to Bill.

'No reason why not. She's got to go out this afternoon anyway, because I've decided to buy a tape recorder. It could be useful for dictating letters when Noni's not around. What do you think of the idea, Sarah?'

'I'm terribly sorry but I just can't stay and talk,' Sarah said. 'I'm on duty, you see.'

'Oh, well, ring up again, my dear. I enjoy our little chats. Or better still, come round and see me. When's your duty day off, Sarah? Wednesday, isn't it? Come and see me on Wednesday.'

'I'm back on the ward now. I don't know if . . .'

'Tell Matron I said so . . . no, don't bother, I'll ring her and ask her as a favour. She'll fix it if I ask. You run along, my dear, and I'll see you soon.'

Sarah replaced the receiver. The palms of her hands were damp with nerves.

'I don't know what time, but Noni's coming this afternoon.'

'Which nurse is on the private rooms?'

'Sister Tafferty, I think.'

'Then tell her she is to send Mrs Brisbane down here. No, Noni might not come. I'll see the hall porter at Reception myself!'

Sarah turned to go. Their eyes met, Sarah holding a mute appeal for at least a word of forgiveness, but Bill's face was completely impassive.

'I'm sorry!' she said once more, and turning, went out of the room with a defeated air.

Bill hurried down to Reception where he left the most explicit instructions for the porter to phone him the moment Mrs Brisbane walked in through the doors. He tried, without it appearing to be a personal matter, to impress on the man that it was of the utmost importance that she did not come into the hospital unnoticed. He wondered whether a fiver might ensure that the man really took note of who came into the building, but decided it would look very odd.

He went out for a hurried lunch at the

Chequers, but left most of the sandwiches untouched, just in case Noni had had an even earlier lunch and arrived at the hospital before him. Consequently, he had a long, two-hour wait in his office, which seemed three times as long. His eyes kept going to the phone. It remained stubbornly silent. At half-past two, afraid he might have missed her, he rang down to Reception and, struggling to keep his voice casual, told the porter he was back in his office and waiting to hear when Mrs Brisbane came in.

It wasn't until half-past three that the phone rang and the hall porter told him that Noni had just gone upstairs in the lift.

Bill slammed down the receiver and, no longer caring what anyone he passed might think of his behaviour, ran the length of the corridor and took the single flight of stairs up to the suite of private rooms. As he turned the corner on the landing he saw Noni stepping out of the lift ahead of him. He waited for the lift gates to close and then hurried forward and took her arm.

'Noni!'

She turned and stared at him as if he were a ghost.

'It's Saturday!' she said stupidly. 'I was so sure you wouldn't be here.'

The sight of her brought a strange choking

lump to his throat. For a moment or two, he couldn't speak. Then he said simply:

'Oh, I do love you so!'

A look of acute pain came into her eyes.

'Bill, don't!'

He got himself under control and attempted a smile.

'I know why you are here. There isn't a parcel. I got Sarah to phone because I simply had to see you.'

'Bill, we agreed . . . '

'Yes, yes I know, but something has happened. I can't tell you here. Come down to my office.'

She knew she ought to refuse. The only hope she had of making her marriage work was if the break with Bill were absolute — final. But the sight of him was weakening her, just as it had weakened him. With his hand gripping her arm, she realized just how starved she had been for a sight of him, for the sound of his voice — to hear him say: *I do love you so.*

She had no strength to argue with him. He was hurrying her down the stairs and along the corridor to his office. A couple of young nurses passed them, smiled at Bill, looked curiously at Noni. Then they were alone, the door closed behind them.

The next moment they were in each other's

arms. It was contrary to either of their intentions, but they were powerless to prevent the instinctive need to be close, to be kissing one another as if all the kissing they would ever do had to be crowded into this split second of time. But even as he pressed his mouth hungrily against hers, Bill could not forget why she was here. He pushed her very gently away from him and taking a deep breath said:

'Noni, what I have to tell you is pretty grim. Sarah came to see me this morning. She told Philip about us!'

'Yes, I guessed it must be her!'

He looked at her astonished, trying to fathom her expression.

'Then you knew? Brisbane said something to you? *How did he take it?*'

Noni turned her face away from him. She didn't want to talk about it. She could never tell Bill what had really happened. He didn't know Philip — understand him as she did. He wouldn't believe that any man could . . .

'Noni, why don't you say something? What's wrong? Does he want a divorce?'

She forced herself to speak.

'No! And there's nothing for you to worry about, Bill. He was naturally upset but . . . it's all right now.'

Bill stared at her disbelievingly.

'What do you mean, *all right*? How can it be all right? News like that must have knocked him sideways. I could kill Sarah. I very nearly did. He must have been badly hurt. I feel so awful about it, Noni!'

'Don't let's talk about it, Bill. Please believe me, it *is* all right. He took it . . . very well, really. He doesn't think it was anything very . . . very serious. He . . . well, he laughed when I said we had fallen in love.'

'*Laughed*?' Bill took a step forward and caught her arms, looking down at her as if she were out of her mind.

'You don't understand him, Bill. He just doesn't believe in our kind of love. He thinks it's all just romantic nonsense.'

Bill let out his breath.

'You're right, I don't understand. I don't see how any husband can dismiss something like that as . . . as a kind of joke. I don't understand anything any more. I'd have been mad with jealousy — just to think of another man touching you, holding you, loving you . . . the thought of you ever making love with *him* horrifies me.'

She stayed silent, remembering and almost hating Bill for making her remember. It was just as he said — *crazy*. She'd felt no sense of wrong-doing, of guilt, when she'd lain in Bill's arms. What they had shared had seemed then

181

to have no connection with her life with Philip. But now she was feeling guilty because she had allowed her husband to make love to her and had let him force her into an act of unfaithfulness to *Bill*. That really was crazy. A quotation flashed into her mind: '*To Thine own Self be True, Thou Canst not then be false to Any Man*.' Bitterly she reflected that it had not been possible for her to remain 'true to herself'; that would have meant keeping her body for Bill, always and only for him.

'Noni, something's terribly wrong somewhere! You're so quiet. What are you thinking? What has happened to you?'

'Nothing, nothing!' she lied frantically. 'Let me go, Bill. It's so difficult for me to be strong when I'm with you. I must go. Philip will be wondering where I am. I don't think I could stand it if he started to accuse me of being with you. I ought not to be here. It's too dangerous.'

'Dangerous?' Once again, Bill picked up the leading word. 'How can it be dangerous if he knows about us and is treating it as a joke? Wasn't that true? You're hiding something from me, Noni. What *is* going on?'

Desperately she fumbled for words. She had not wanted to tell him but she had to make him see that it wasn't safe any more for them to meet.

'Philip has threatened to have you struck off the register and ruin your career,' she breathed the words. 'If that happened, I should blame myself all my life. So for my sake, Bill, let me go.'

'Then let him. I want him to divorce you,' Bill said roughly. 'You're not going to stop him if he wants a divorce, Noni?'

'But he doesn't,' she cried desperately. 'It was only a threat. He wants me to stay with him and I'm going to, so there's no point in giving him cause to try to ruin you. Maybe he can't anyway. It doesn't make any difference because I *have* to stay with him.'

'No, you don't have to. You *want* to.'

She looked at him now, seeing the hurt bewilderment in his eyes. He did not mean to but he was making things so much harder for her. She restrained the almost irresistible urge to go to him, put her arms round him and comfort him. Instead she said gently:

'Yes, I *want* to stay with him — not because I love him; I'll never be able to love anyone but you, Bill — but because I'm his wife and he's in trouble. It isn't just a question of martyrdom or being noble or anything like that. It's just that I couldn't live with myself if I did what I want and you want, regardless. I know you understand that. Deep down, you feel the same. If we were different people, Bill — if we were selfish people who could ignore the rest of humanity, then we might have been able to share our lives and even enjoy them. But that's not us — not you and not me.'

He was sitting at his desk, his elbows on the polished surface, his hands covering his face. He wanted to shout at her, to tell her that she was wrong, that they had something fine and good and predestined and that it was right for them to treasure and keep it *at any cost*. But he could not. In a way, she was stronger than he. If she asked him now to take her away from Philip and make her his own, he could not have refused her. He sat silently fighting that strength of hers. But he would not argue with her. Deeper even than his love for her was his respect for her ideals. In the long run, he knew he could not find happiness without an ideal to live up to. To abandon all that was finer in human thinking was to reduce man to little more than an animal. Noni was right — neither of them could love the other if they gave way to extreme selfishness. The very qualities they had discovered in each other and loved, were now barriers which must separate them.

He took his hands away from his face, wanting to tell her that he understood, that he loved her more than ever; but Noni had already gone. He jumped up, about to follow her. But he sat down again. Noni was right in this, too. Neither of them could have stood the strain of another 'good-bye'.

He sat there for a long time, staring into the gathering shadows, half hoping she would return, yet knowing with completely certainty that she would never come back to this room again.

11

Noni stood by the fireplace staring at the Christmas cards aligned on the mantelpiece. There was the usual floral effort from Sydney and Eileen with whom she had been spending ten days whilst Philip was in London having his operation. There was a minute Father Christmas card from young Micky with whom she had spent so much of her time and in whose company she had found a measure of happiness. She would have liked to have brought him home with her but it was impossible with Philip due back; a young boy around the house would be the last thing he would want.

There were cards from old school friends, her father, Philip's parents and from most of the hospital staff of doctors, Matron and one or two of the nurses, including Sarah Bristow. But no card from Bill. Each time the postman came, she would hurriedly glance at the envelopes, looking for Bill's writing, yet knowing all the time that there wouldn't be any word from him. Their break had been complete.

For a whole month, she had neither seen

nor heard from him. The only news she had was from Sarah Bristow when she had come to tea on her day off on two occasions before Philip went off to London. Sarah had come at Philip's request and she seemed to be the only person who could put him in a really good humour. From Sarah he obtained the news of hospital activities and he would become animated and interested. Each time Sarah left and Noni showed her to the door, Sarah turned to Noni and said:

'I see Bill Aden around. He's always very busy but he seems to keep well.'

These snippets of news were all Noni had to cling to. She wondered if Sarah likewise passed on news of her to Bill. Maybe he was already beginning to forget her. She hoped that he was not unhappy and yet, perversely, she could not bear the thought that he might have been able to put her out of his life so quickly and easily!

Sarah's visits had a peculiar effect upon Noni as well as a therapeutic effect upon Philip. Noni could never look on the older girl as anything but an enemy after what she had done. But for Sarah, Philip would not have known about Bill, or have had the opportunity to make odd, sarcastic remarks about what he called 'her affair'. Each time he referred to the past in this way it was like a knife twisting in a still open wound. He always seemed to enjoy her discomfort — to derive a sadistic satisfaction when she attempted to change the conversation.

'Good God, Noni, can't you take a bit of teasing?' he would say. But, steel herself though she might, she never failed to react with a stiffening of her muscles or a rush of colour to her cheeks, and therefore Philip continued to jibe when he had nothing better to do. Once he had made a cutting remark about Bill in Sarah's presence. Sarah had said quietly:

'Bill Aden is a first-class psychiatrist and a nice person. I don't think you should speak of him like that!'

Strangely, Philip had accepted the rebuke. Noni, whilst still not liking Sarah, had, nevertheless, been grateful to her for championing Bill as well as for passing on in private what news she had of him. Noni realized that Sarah was trying to be friendly, perhaps hoping to make up for her betrayal. She tried to be generous and to like the nurse, but she could not. She knew she would never trust Sarah again; and without trust there could be no genuine affection.

After Philip had gone to London, Noni knew she would go completely to pieces from sheer loneliness if she stayed in the house with only Mrs Reeves for company. She desperately needed one good friend but because of the circumstances of her life there was no one with whom she was on such intimate terms that she could turn to them now. The wives of Philip's colleagues were, for the most part, much older than Noni. Many of them had been nurses before they were married and Noni had little in common with them. The younger wives kept their distance because of the reputation Philip had held in the hospital — of being autocratic and critical of his juniors. Because their husbands did not like Philip, the wives made no effort to include Noni in their circle.

So there was no one except Eileen. Noni packed a suitcase and went off to Berkshire to stay with her. Eileen had been sympathetic even though she did not understand fully the depth of her younger sister's love for Bill or the emptiness of Noni's life now that she had parted from him.

'What you need is a child, Noni,' Eileen suggested. 'I've said so before and I'm even more sure of it now. A child would bring you and Philip together again, and you're so good with children. I sometimes think Micky loves you even more than he loves me.'

'Philip doesn't want children!'

'I know he did not *in the past*, but he

189

might now, especially as you say there's really no hope of him being able to continue with his surgery.'

'But *I* don't want a child now, Eileen — not any more; not *Philip's* child . . . ' Sydney had been maddeningly prosaic.

'If you ask me, Noni,' he said to his sister-in-law who had not invited his opinion, 'this is the best thing that could have happened. It has put an end, once and for all, to an affair which was at best hopeless and at worst very dangerous indeed.'

'It was not hopeless!' Noni was stung to reply. 'Bill and I were going to ask Philip for a divorce; we were going to be married.'

'And suppose Philip had refused a divorce? He might have done, you know. Men in his position don't like any scandal attached to their names, even if they are innocent of wrongdoing themselves. And what about your young man's career? Philip might have taken it into his head to ruin him. No, it was a thoroughly unsatisfactory business, Noni, and you're well out of it. I know this accident is a terrible thing but at least it has brought you to your senses. You've just got to buckle down and make a fresh start. Forget the other fellow.'

Yes, it was easy for Sydney to talk in his pompous way. He saw life entirely through the eyes of a solicitor. He was devoted to Eileen and his son and his limited capacity to love them was enough for Eileen whose romantic side came very much second to that of the domestic housewife she was at heart. Eileen only required her man to be kind, good and affectionate. She did not need a communion of the spirit or a 'lover'; she just wanted a husband, a head of the house, a provider.

Noni realized that she herself had not been so different before Bill had entered her life. She had known a vague loneliness of spirit and an unaccountable lack of something in her marriage, without being able to give it a name. She had almost believed Philip when he had tried to convince her that there was no such thing as 'love' except in books and plays and poetry; that 'love' was just a figment of people's imagination; or that if it existed, it was only for the few.

She might have been happier if she had never known that it could and did exist. But never, at any time, did she regret what had happened between her and Bill. It was the most important, the most precious and the most enduring of all the memories she had or ever would have now.

Her week with Eileen went by quickly — too quickly. She was happier away from her own home, away from the vicinity of the hospital where she was conscious all the time of Bill's proximity. She wondered if Bill felt this, too; if he would ask for a transfer to another hospital. It was so hard to forget him, knowing that she might turn a corner of the street in the town and come face to face with him or walk into a shop and see him there. She longed for such an encounter and yet knew she ought not to want it to happen. A meeting could only make things harder for them both.

'It'll get better in time!' were Eileen's parting words as Noni packed her suitcase to go home.

But it was not proving so.

It was nearly Christmas and Philip was coming home — a Philip she had not seen since his operation because he had said he did not wish her to visit him. She was not with him when Seagrave told him his operating days were finished.

Seagrave had told her on the telephone that Philip had taken it badly, but that was only to be expected. The vital question was, how badly? Despite Herod's and Seagrave's warnings that the operation would do no more than restore the barest minimum of vision, Philip had continued to discuss the future in terms of 'When I get down to work again!' It was as if he were trying to will the truth to be otherwise, as if he felt that by not admitting to it the fact would not exist. Now the operation was over and he had been forced to accept the truth.

In the morning he would be here. And in the afternoon, the Local Authority was sending one of their home teachers to see him. Noni had spoken to the woman, a Mrs Dartry, on the telephone.

'I'm afraid I shan't be able to get along more than once or twice a week,' she said said to Noni. 'We are very short-staffed and I have a great many other blind people in my area to visit.'

'If it's difficult for you, please don't trouble until you have more time!' Noni replied politely. The woman had laughed.

'My dear, I must come. It is essential that your husband's rehabilitation begin at once — the sooner the better.'

'Rehabilitation?'

'Yes! I can start him on Braille for one thing. Then as soon as there is a vacancy, he will be sent to America Lodge in Torquay.'

Mrs Dartry had gone on to explain about this rehabilitation centre for blind persons. Philip would be taught there to adjust himself to the world of the sightless — to walk without bending or shuffling; to shave himself, to deal with food on a plate — in short, to become as independent as possible. There would also be lessons at which he would continue with his Braille, learn to type if he wished and be taught various hobbies.

Noni felt it all sounded very encouraging. Philip would not after all have to find time, so priceless in the past, suddenly lying heavy on his hands. There would be a great deal he could still do.

Philip, however, had other ideas. Whilst by no means broken in spirit, he arrived home filled with bitterness and an iron determination not to discuss his future at all. When Noni told him Mrs Dartry was coming, he refused even to see her. He made Noni telephone to cancel the appointment, but by a stroke of luck, Mrs Dartry was out and would not be back in her office before her appointment with Philip at half-past two.

'You can tell her when she comes that I've no wish to see her,' he told Noni and became angry when she tried to argue with him that this was not only silly, in view of how much she would be able to help him, but rude, too.

Mrs Dartry, fortunately, was more than understanding when an embarrassed Noni made her explanations at the front door. She was a grey-haired middle-aged woman, a widow who had spent the last thirty years of her life dealing with the newly-blind.

'You leave your husband to me, my dear!' she said to Noni. 'I'll soon talk some sense into him.'

'It seems so much worse for him than for other people!' Noni said sadly. 'His career meant everything and now — well it has ceased to exist — just because of the carelessness of a bad driver.'

'My dear Mrs Brisbane,' Mrs Dartry replied in her quiet, steady voice, 'to each person, his plight seems worse than that of others, but believe me, there are a hundred cases I could put to you this minute which are even more tragic than that of your husband. I gather, for one thing, that there are no financial worries in this instance? Although there are grants for the blind, where there is a financial necessity, it is one of the biggest steps towards rehabilitation if a man can go on supporting his wife and family unaided.'

Promising to have another talk with Noni after she had seen Philip, Mrs Dartry calmly walked into his room. Noni, outside the door, heard Philip's voice, angry and dictatorial. She hurried away to the kitchen to make a cup of tea, believing that poor Mrs Dartry would shortly emerge badly in need of one. It was, however, over half an hour before she reappeared, smiling.

Noni looked at her calm face with surprise.

'Don't look so terrified, Mrs Brisbane!' the older woman said laughing. 'He didn't eat me, although he was a little difficult. A man with a lot of determination! But he wouldn't have gotten where he did as a surgeon without it, would he?'

She accepted the tea Noni offered and went on:

'We had a long talk about the future. Personally, I can't see any reason at all why he shouldn't eventually take on a job as an adviser to B.P.A.S. We discussed the possibilities fully. Mr Brisbane gave me a run-down on what such work entails and there is nothing, other than the transport to and from his place of work, which would prevent him from doing it.'

Noni breathed a long sigh of relief.

'That's marvellous!' she cried. 'It would mean everything to Philip to get back to medicine again.'

'I'm sure that is the answer — if we can get him to consider it.'

'You mean, he won't . . . ?'

'Are you so surprised that he won't even talk about such work in connection with himself? Our discussion was purely hypothetical, of course. I asked him for his advice

196

about such work for a blind person — call it a little trick I used if you like. At the moment, he says if he can't be a surgeon, he won't be anything! But that will wear off, I'm sure of it. The idea will be in his mind and he has consented to learn Braille. We can't force a person to learn if they don't wish, you know!'

Noni leaned forward eagerly.

'Perhaps I could help him? Couldn't I learn, too? Then if the time came when he wanted to write notes for his work, I could take them down in Braille and he would be able to read them back. I do so want to help him in any way I can, Mrs Dartry.'

'I know!' The woman looked at Noni sympathetically. 'It isn't easy for you as his wife to sit back and do nothing, but you know, you mustn't try to help him too much. For you to learn Braille with him is an excellent idea, but it would be wrong for you to give way to the desire to do everything for him. It would end up with him becoming completely dependent on you and he would hate that — and you, too, in all probability. Let him try to do things for himself as much as possible. Only help when you have to.'

Noni could understand the good sense of this. But would Philip see it this way? He was used to giving orders — he wasn't going to like the new position he would be in — that of a pupil having to learn how to live all over again. Had he the courage and the will to go back to the bottom rung of the ladder?

When Mrs Dartry left, Noni went into Philip's room. He was sitting in a chair by the window, his face turned away from her. Pity for him engulfed her and she went over to place her hands on his shoulders and lean her cheek against the back of his head. She felt him stiffen beneath her touch and as he turned, his fair skin coloured an angry red.

'I thought I told you I didn't want to see that woman!'

She removed her hands quickly, flushing nervously.

'I'm sorry, Philip. I did tell her that you didn't wish to see her, but she just walked in.'

'Damned impertinence!' His tone softened a little. 'All the same, I suppose I might as well learn Braille. It could come in useful, if only for reading. As for writing up my notes, I can use the tape recorder.'

'Your notes, Philip?'

'Well, you don't think I'm going to sit here doing nothing morning, noon and night, do you? I'm working on a sort of autobiography of all my more interesting cases. It could become a useful text book for students. Seagrave suggested it and it gives me something to do.'

'It sounds a wonderful idea!' Noni said encouragingly. 'Maybe you could use the notes when you start lecturing . . . ' She broke off, remembering Mrs Dartry's warning that Philip had been unwilling even to contemplate such a career.

'Ha!' said Philip. 'So that woman was brain-washing you, too, was she? Just who does she think I am — *me*, doing a deskbound job. No, thank you very much. I'm damned if I'll descend to *that* level.'

Afraid that she might do more harm than good by trying to argue with him, Noni let the subject drop. But she wished she had not when Philip, changing the subject again, said:

'Well, did you see the boy-friend while I was away?'

'Philip!'

He laughed, restored to good humour as always when she rose to what he now termed 'the bait'.

'Can't take a bit of teasing, can you, Noni?'

She turned away and her hands gripped the edge of the table, her knuckles white.

'I can't see that it is anything to joke about, Philip.'

'I'm well aware of that, but I do. You surely don't expect me to take your little skirmish *seriously*, do you?'

'Perhaps not!' Noni said tightly. 'Perhaps

I'm being silly to let my conscience bother me. I know it must seem strange, coming from me, but I took my marriage very seriously, Philip. I think marriage *is* serious. If one makes vows in church, one should at least be sorry if one is weak enough to break them.'

Philip shrugged his shoulders.

'Well, if you're worrying on my account, don't. I don't hold it against you. Just so long as you aren't still being unfaithful, I'm prepared to forgive and forget.'

'*I know you have forgiven me, Philip, but you won't forget!*' Noni cried from her heart. '*You keep alluding to . . . to Bill. Every time you do, you make me remember him.*' Suddenly she was on her knees beside her husband, her hands held out supplicatingly towards him. 'Please, Philip, try to understand. I want our marriage to work. I want us to have a completely fresh start together, to begin again from the beginning. If we could do that, then we could be happy together, build something worthwhile out of our lives. Maybe . . . maybe if you really wanted it, we could have children, make ourselves into a family . . . '

She had not meant to say so much, had not even known what she was going to say before the words poured out, begging him to help her because she wanted so desperately to be able to help him.

'A family? Good God, no. That's the last thing I want. And you'll have quite enough on your hands looking after me. As to making a 'fresh start', I really don't know what you are talking about. Start what again? What's the matter with the way our marriage is at the moment?'

She could not speak. *He simply did not understand.* He did not realize that he had very nearly lost her. He could not see that she was desperately unhappy, desperately lonely and anxious to get nearer to him. He was blissfully ignorant of the fact that anything at all was wrong other than his own misfortune.

'Well, are you going to explain what's wrong with our marriage?'

She stood up and walked away from him.

'I can't explain,' she whispered. 'I expect I'm just talking nonsense, anyway. Forget it, Philip. I'll go and get your tea.'

He heard her leave the room, heard the door close quietly after her. He shrugged his shoulders, sighing. Noni was far too emotional these days. A pity she hadn't a bit more of Sarah Bristow's jolliness. He could do with cheering up. He must ring the hospital, tell Sarah he was back and she must come and visit him on her day off.

He switched on his tape recorder and forgot Noni and Sarah as he listened with growing pleasure to the sound of his own voice as the tape played it back.

12

Bill was fighting a battle with himself. He'd sworn that he would not speak to Sarah Bristow again after she had betrayed Noni and him to Philip. But now word had got back to him through the hospital grapevine that Sarah had been visiting the Brisbanes and he was desperately tempted to get in touch with her. Anything would be better than this complete absence of news of Noni.

He knew, of course, from Harvey, what was happening to Philip. He knew the operation had failed to restore his sight just as Herod had predicted; he knew Philip was going to the rehabilitation centre at Torquay as soon as there was a vacancy. He knew Philip had rung Harvey and had a long discussion with him about the possibilities of becoming a lecturer in one of the training colleges. But of Noni he knew nothing.

He had tried hard enough to forget her. He'd been away to stay with friends. Because he was an eligible bachelor and, at thirty-two, of an age to marry and settle down, most of his friends' wives had produced eligible young women for him to meet and get to know in their houses. There'd been one girl in particular — a fair-haired blue-eyed young journalist who had reminded him of Noni. For a little while, he had been interested in this girl who looked so like her; he'd taken her out to lunch and on to the races and out to dinner afterwards. But as the hours had gone by, it had become more and more apparent that however like Noni the girl might look, she was the complete opposite in every other way. She was amusing enough, with a quick, ready wit and a keen intelligence, but beneath the feminine exterior lay a hard, calculating core which had soon begun to grate on his nerves. He'd had a hard job extricating himself from the finale the girl seemed to expect. He had cut a date with her and thought that he would not hear from her again. But she had telephoned him twice. Each time, he had pleaded an overload of work and finally she had taken the hint.

Looking back on the episode, he could almost laugh at himself if the reason behind it were not so tragic. A year ago, he would have given the girl what she wanted, even enjoyed what she had to offer, and probably have forgotten all about her. Now she remained in his mind as a strange symbol of his complete detachment from the world around him. Only in his work could he lose himself and, for a few hours a day, forget about Noni.

Other members of the hospital staff noticed the change in him.

'You're very quiet these days, Bill. Feeling okay?'

One after the other, they'd eyed him anxiously, with similar comments. He was now convinced his inner unhappiness could be seen on his face although when he looked in the mirror, he could see no change in himself. He wondered if he should ask for a transfer — get right away from the district and all its painful memories. He wanted to go and yet his patients held him. There were so many who had been under his treatment for months on end; and there was Robert, who now came as an out-patient. He could not leave them in the lurch for his own peace of mind. Or perhaps deep down in his subconscious, he realized that running away from the scene would not bring the peace he craved. If he were going to readjust himself to life without Noni, then he had to do so here.

His hand hesitantly lay on the telephone. To ring Sarah or not?

He smiled grimly. He might as well; he must have intended to do so all along. Why else had he inquired of his own nurse this morning what ward Sarah was now on!

He lifted the receiver and asked for the

extension number.

Sarah sounded more than a little surprised when he asked her to meet him at the Chequers that evening for a drink.

'It's nice of you to ask me, Bill, but I don't know if I can. This is my half-day and this afternoon I'm having tea with the Brisbanes . . . ' Her voice trailed off uncertainly.

'That's okay . . . it doesn't matter what time. I'll be at the bar sometime after six-thirty. You come along and join me when you can!'

He put down the phone and found his hands trembling. He needed only Sarah's casual reference to the Brisbanes to put him in this state. He must somehow get himself under control or *he'd* be needing psychiatric treatment himself!

He awaited Sarah's coming that evening with more impatience than, as a young boy, he had awaited his first date. He knew it was madness to give way so completely but his will no longer had the power to control his mind. He knew that whatever Sarah had to tell him, he could not be happier for it. If Noni were ill or unhappy, *he* would be even more wretched. If she were well and happy, then he would be miserable because she was so soon able to forget him.

Nevertheless, he waited. At a quarter to

seven, he caught sight of Sarah's red head as she made her way through the now crowded room towards the bar.

She greeted him a little uneasily. Since the time when she'd been to his room to confess that she had told Philip, Bill had cut her. If she passed him in the corridor, he looked away and did not speak to her. She believed he hated her and accepted it as only fair. She had done a pretty rotten thing to him. Now, suddenly he was inviting her out. She was curious and yet afraid to know the reason.

Bill did not beat about the bush. He ordered their drinks and shouldered a way through the crowd to a moderately quiet table.

'I want to know how Noni is. I presume you've seen her?'

She would have had to be all kinds of a fool not to have seen the unhappiness in his eyes; not to have guessed that he was as deeply in love with Noni Brisbane as ever. The first instinctive twinge of jealousy gave way to pity. She could guess what it must have cost him to have to ask *her* this.

'She's all right, Bill. I think she has lost a lot of weight, but she isn't ill.'

'Is she happy?'

His eyes were searching her face. She looked down at her drink and said:

'I don't know. I can't answer that. She doesn't very often smile. I don't think I've heard her laugh.'

'And *he* . . . her husband. What's he like to her?'

Again Sarah hesitated. She did not want to hurt Bill — to make him any more unhappy. Her desire for revenge had been short-lived and now she felt only pity for him. No one knew better than she the torments into which love could plunge a person. Bill was caught and he was suffering and she was sorry.

'Well, answer me, Sarah. Please!'

'He . . . he's inclined to be irritable. You see, Noni can't hide her feelings — she shows that she is sorry for him. She can't hit back when he's being difficult and he needs someone to stand up to him.'

As I do! she thought. She gave him tit for tat. If he barked at her, she barked back and that made him laugh. He wasn't intentionally unkind to Noni. But she got on his nerves and he was too self-centred a man to control himself. She'd seen Noni hurt and even humiliated when Philip spoke roughly to her in Sarah's presence.

'He always was a bit of a bully!' Bill said bitterly.

'But he doesn't *know* he's bullying!' Sarah defended Philip.

'Then someone should tell him. Noni ought not to be living with him . . . ' he broke off, realizing what he was saying. Sarah put a hand on his arm.

'You're bound to think that way because you love her.'

Bill gave Sarah a long look of bitterness.

'There's not much point in denying it to *you*, is there, Sarah? Anyway, it's a relief to be able to talk about Noni to someone. Yes, I love her. I don't know if she knows just *how much* I love her. I can't get her out of my mind. I can't sleep for thinking about her and when I do sleep, I dream of her. It's sheer hell!'

'I know!' Sarah said softly. 'I loved someone once like that. It was just as hopeless for me as it is for you. But time does help, Bill. I don't say one ever forgets — I never have — but it helps. I've learned to live my life without him.'

'Have you, Sarah? And what kind of life is it? You aren't happy. You go from one man to another trying to find what you lost in someone else. But you never have, have you? You never have found *him* again.'

The look on her face stilled him.

'Damn you for saying that!' She downed her drink and the eyes she lifted to Bill were bright with tears. 'But since this is an evening for home truths, so it seems, I'll do my confessing too. No, I've never found anyone I could love as I loved him. I know I never will. I don't want to love anyone like that again. I don't think I could anyway. I'm harder, tougher, a different person. Just as you will be different — are different! Just as Noni Brisbane will be different. We all change with our experiences. You should know that, Bill. You're the psychiatrist.'

'I'm sorry, Sarah. I didn't mean to hurt you!'

His voice was gentle. She smiled at him.

'No more than I — the real me — intended to hurt you or Noni. Most of us want to strike back at someone, something, when we get hurt. Forget it, Bill. Let's talk about Noni — I know that's why you asked me here.'

'There's so much I want to know but what's the point? Now that you are here and I can talk about her, suddenly I don't want to know. I'm afraid to know. The thought that she is only a few miles away is almost too much for me. I can't even drown my sorrows . . . ' He gave a wry smile. 'If I get tight I might jump in the car and drive to her house. Tell me, Sarah, what's your role there? Is it Noni or Philip who invites you? Why do you go?'

Sarah shrugged.

'I'm not sure. Philip invites me . . . he says I do him good and I think that's true. He . . . he was very generous to me when he left the hospital after I'd been his nurse. Maybe I feel I owe him something. Maybe he interests me. I don't know.'

'Interests you — as a man or as a medical case?'

'Both!'

Bill looked at her curiously.

'Then you find him attractive?'

'In a way, I suppose. 'Interesting' is probably nearer the mark. He isn't like anyone I've met before. One has the feeling about him that whatever he had decided to become, he would have succeeded. I think if he had made up his mind to become Prime Minister, he would have made the grade just as surely as he achieved such incredible heights in surgery. One has to respect as well as admire him.'

'Anyone can get to the top if he is ruthless enough. He was never liked in the hospital; admired and feared — but never liked.'

'Are successful people ever popular amongst their own kind?' Sarah countered. 'There's bound to be jealousy, envy — and you have an added reason to dislike him.'

Bill was silent for a moment. Then he said: 'I don't dislike him for any other reason than that he failed to make Noni happy. I could stand this being apart from Noni if I could only believe he loved her, or even that he valued her.'

Now it was Sarah's turn to hesitate. Reluctantly, she said:

'I think he does value her. She's more to him than you might think, Bill. He is a self-made man but Noni does quite naturally all the things he has had to learn to do. She is exactly the kind of wife he wanted. Her home is beautiful, she is beautiful, other men like and admire her.'

'You mean she is his prize possession!'

'Perhaps in a way. He knows she is on a level above his own and he wants to keep her there. I think what I am trying to say is that he is proud of her.'

'Even when she was unfaithful to him?'

'I don't think that bothered him one tiny bit as much as it bothered Noni. Philip refused to take it seriously. He even joked about you and Noni in front of me.'

'Oh, God, my poor Noni!' Bill whispered. 'How she must have hated it.'

'Yes. But if she is to go on living with him, maybe it's better that way. If he'd reacted like a normal husband, she might have been even more unhappy. Jealousy isn't easy to live with. Philip isn't the least jealous of you. It would

212

never enter his head that Noni might leave *him* for you. Ergo, he isn't jealous.'

'Well, I'm jealous — so much so that I can't bear to think of her with him. Tell me, Sarah, what does she do with herself?'

'Looks after him; reads to him. She's learning Braille with him and she writes letters for him. One day she went down to Torquay to see America House, the rehabilitation centre where he's going. That was on my day off so I could be with him while she was away. She came back madly enthusiastic about it. I gather they have all the best equipment. The staff are wonderful and she was terribly impressed with the atmosphere of the place. Everyone mixed freely and helped each other. She thinks Philip will like it there.'

'Will Noni go there with him?'

'Apparently not — the idea is to get away from the family and learn to stand on your own feet. I think Noni is going to stay with her sister.'

Bill had never seen Eileen but he'd seen snaps of her. She was short and plump and, apart from blue eyes and fair hair, not in the least like Noni, who resembled their mother. He'd seen snaps of her, too — a tall, fair slim woman with Noni's eyes. She was half Norwegian, but Noni had never known her as she died when Noni was born. Eileen took more after their father, the Brigadier. Noni had talked about him a great deal and Bill had sometimes though that he and Philip were two of a kind. Perhaps that was why Noni had married Philip — a sort of father complex. The old man was retired now and lived on his own pension too far away for Noni to see him very often although she did try to visit him at least twice a year. No doubt Noni would take the opportunity to see him during the three months Philip was away.

There was little more Sarah could tell him. Bill bought her another drink and soon afterwards she left. He, too, should have been going home, but he put off the inevitable moment. Alone in his flat, he would start thinking of Noni. He glanced round the room and saw a doctor friend. Without really desiring his company, Bill nevertheless went over and joined him. Anyone was better company than his own thoughts and might help him to forget Noni if only for a little while.

13

Sarah sat in the lounge of the Preston Hotel on the seafront in Torquay and looked once more at the clock. It was nearly two-thirty. Philip's letter had told her to meet him here at three. She was still very uncertain if she were doing the right thing by coming. When his first letter had come asking her to get leave and visit him at once, she had thought it would be impossible, even if she had wanted to do so. Matron didn't like having sudden requests for leave sprung on her. However, as most of the people had wanted to be away over Christmas and New Year, Matron had given her consent. She had written to tell him so and asked him to explain why he wished to see her.

Philip had refused to comment. Both his letters were short and had obviously been dictated to someone at the rehabilitation centre, so they were deliberately impersonal and vague.

'Do try and get leave and come down to Torquay. The weather is very mild and I think you would enjoy it here. There are

215

one or two family matters I would like to discuss with you. Arrange it if you can . . . '

His second letter had been even more brief:

'I will meet you after lunch (about three p.m.) in the lounge of the Preston Hotel where I have booked a room for you.'

'Family matters' might mean anything or nothing. Noni was staying with her sister so it could hardly concern *her*. Nor did Sarah think that this was a 'proposition' from Philip. Although he flirted with her in a jovial way when she visited him at his home, he never went beyond the point of allowing her to know he found her attractive. There'd been no attempts to hold her hand or to behave in a way which might indicate he wanted their strange friendship to develop further. As far as Sarah knew, Noni remained the only woman of interest to him in his life.

So what am I doing here? she asked herself the same question she had asked on the long train journey down. *Nothing better to do, probably, combined with a free holiday.* But why did he so particularly wish to see *her*? Sarah had surprised herself by coming when there was no really good reason for using up a whole week's leave in what promised to be a rather dull hotel. Maybe Philip had managed to touch the inescapable streak of curiosity in her nature which had so often in the past led her to do the improbable *'just to see what it's like!'*

The door of the lounge opened and the hall porter led Philip over to the corner of the room where she was sitting. One or two of the residents looked up curiously at the approaching blind man but politely dropped their eyes again.

Sarah stod up and held out her hand.

'Hullo, Philip. How are you?'

'Am I glad to see you!' Philip greeted her, settling into the chair beside her. 'I've been on tenterhooks all morning in case you decided not to come.' He gave a sudden laugh. 'I had a hell of a job fixing it! In case you don't know, Sarah, you're my long lost aunt over from Australia. They don't approve of friends visiting while we're at the centre. It's supposed to have a bad effect or something. So, Aunt Sarah, how are you looking, I wonder? As beautiful as ever?'

'Really, Philip, how can I answer that!'

She was suddenly very pleased to see him. He looked distinguished in a well-cut dark check suit. She noticed suddenly that his hair was beginning to silver at the temples. It suited him — made him look the aristocrat he was not.

'*You* are looking very handsome!' she said. 'And now, tell me why you wanted me to come? I've been half dead with curiosity.'

'I'll explain why I need you, Sarah. I've decided to bypass this place,' Philip said frowning. 'We're supposed to do everything for ourselves — even tidy our own bedrooms. I ask you, Sarah, me having to learn to be a skivvy! Well, I've put my foot down . . . I'm damned if I'll do such things. They don't seem to realize the position I held as a surgeon. They treat me like everyone else!'

Sarah laughed at his tone. He sounded like a disgruntled little boy.

'It's all very well for you to laugh, my girl!' Philip went on indignantly. 'Do you know 'They' want me to learn pottery! They seem to think because I was a surgeon I might have the ability to model things in filthy clay. Learning Braille is one thing — I don't object to that or even having to learn to walk upright; that makes sense. But the rest of it, oh, no! I've quite made up my mind that I shall take up lecturing. I don't imagine I shall enjoy it particularly but at least it has some connections with my old work. So I want *you* to do some telephoning for me — I've listed the names of some people who might pull a few strings and make appointments for me to

see them in London, *this* week. You can take
me up to Town from here. I've just got to get
a job off my own bat. They keep telling me
down here that I must wait until I'm
readjusted. What about it, Sarah?'

'Okay, if that's what you want!'

Philip reached out a hand and gripped her
arm.

'I knew you'd do it, Sarah. I knew I could
count on you. I telephoned Noni, you know,
and asked *her* to help me but she wouldn't.
Had the impertinence to tell me that I ought
to stick it out at the centre, and co-operate.
That Mrs Dartry convinced her it would be
in my own interest to do so. As if she can
decide what is best for me! I told Noni I
would never forgive her but she wouldn't
change her mind — kept on about it being for
my own good.'

'She's probably right!' Sarah said thoughtfully.

Unexpectedly, Philip was not annoyed.

'None of that matters now you have said
you're willing to help me. I can do a lecturing
job standing on my head. Don't you see,
Sarah, I've all the knowledge I need stored up
in my mind. I don't need to be able to *see* to
lecture to a class of students.'

'You may want to refer to your notes.'

'I've thought of that. That's the other

reason I wanted you down here. This is where you come in. Would you be willing to pack up your job, Sarah, and let me employ you as a kind of nurse-cum-private secretary? You've had a medical training. You'd be able to follow my notes — I can put them on tape and you can type them out. With *you* beside me, I can cope, I know I can, and I'd pay you well. What about it, Sarah?'

She hesitated. Philip sounded so sure he would succeed, she didn't really doubt him. But she needed time to think it over. Was she willing to throw in her lot with him? She liked him; he liked her — they got on well together. It could work . . . and she desperately wanted a break from hospital life. It would broaden her horizons; she'd meet new people. It would mean a new interest in life for her, too. But what would Noni have to say? This was what *she* had wanted to do. And Noni was his wife . . .

'Let's discuss my part in it when you've got the job,' she said softly. 'I always think it's a good idea to put first things first. And oughtn't we to talk it over with Noni? She told me she was planning to help you . . . she's learning Braille, isn't she?'

'Yes, she is, but you know as well as I do she'd be no good to me in my work; she was never interested in my surgery. Besides, she hasn't the medical knowledge you have.'

'You've thought it all out then?'

'Yes, I have. I've had a lot of time since my accident to think about my future. At first I thought if I couldn't go back to surgery, I wouldn't want to do another damn thing. But this lecturing . . . well, don't you see, Sarah, it's very closely allied to operating in front of a crowd of students. Any medical foundation should jump at a chance to get a man with my operating experience to lecture for them. I've the experience, the authority, the knowledge.'

Sarah nodded. It was good to see Philip fired with enthusiasm. She certainly didn't intend to be the one to deflate him. She admired his courage. Here, indeed, was a man after her own heart.

'Don't let's waste any more time,' Philip said. 'I'm supposed to be back for tea. There's some blasted social function on this evening. If you get me to the phone, I can make a couple of calls myself. I dared not do it from the centre because you never know who might be listening. I want to present them with a *fait accompli*. I don't want anyone putting a spanner in the works now my mind is made up.'

'You're really very childish, Philip Brisbane,' Sarah said laughing. 'You ought to be concentrating on your basket making or whatever it is you do. I should have thought you'd want to learn to be independent.'

'Why should I?' Philip replied calmly. 'I want to get back to work, Sarah — that's all I'm interested in. Besides, I'm used to having things done for me; I say 'scalpel' and someone hands it to me; 'sutures' and there they are. I can afford to pay someone to wait on me so why not, if it gets me to my objective quicker?'

Now Sarah really understood the single-mindedness of this man. He fastened on a goal and went straight for it. He was not only physically blind but mentally blind to everything that lay on either side of his path. What obstacles he was forced to recognise, he swept aside. She could understand why Bill had called him ruthless. But unlike Bill, she didn't dislike this quality in Philip. Here was a strength stronger than her own, someone who would always be the master of himself and of those around him, too.

She stood up and taking his arm, led him out of the lounge towards the telephone.

When they returned, Philip was triumphant. One appointment at least had been made for him to go for an interview at an important college in two days' time. He was in wonderful spirits.

'I knew it!' he said again and again. 'I knew they'd jump at me. Mark my words, Sarah, I'll get this job. I don't say I'll want to keep it indefinitely, but it'll do for a start. I'm damned grateful to you. You *are* going to help me, aren't you, Sarah?'

'Yes, I am!' She was at one with his mood. 'Even if Noni disapproves?'

'Surely she won't do that. She'll be glad you've got what you want, Philip.'

His tone of voice changed.

'I don't mean about the work. But she may be jealous of *you* personally, Sarah. After all, we'll be thrown together a great deal, you and I. Wives have a way of being jealous, you know.'

Sarah bit her lip. How easy it would be to tell him Noni did not care — that she was still in love with Bill. But she deeply regretted her last betrayal of Noni and she wouldn't do it a second time. Maybe on this occasion she ought to speak out — make Philip realize that his wife was hopelessly in love with another man and would probably welcome her freedom. Philip might turn to her, Sarah, on the re-bound. He'd already said she would be indispensable to him. He might divorce Noni and *marry her*. Then she would be Mrs Philip Brisbane. Blind though Philip might be, he was still a famous man and Sarah did not

223

doubt that he would find a way to remain so. She could do a great deal worse than marry Philip. There were no financial worries. It could all happen . . .

'*But you don't love him,*' she thought, and close after came the bitter reflection: '*You'll never love any other man but the one you lost. You know that, Sarah Brisbane. You've always known it. So why not take this one if you can!*'

There were no obstacles except Philip's feelings for his wife, and her own conscience. She could, but strangely, would not, take the reins in her hands. Philip could find out for himself. This time she would not fight against Fate. But she was still willing to gamble.

'I can't wait to tell Noni about this!' Philip was saying, still deep in his own thoughts. 'That'll make her feel a little less sorry for me. She's too soft-hearted, that's Noni's trouble. Do you know, Sarah, you were quite right about her being unfaithful to me! You tried to retract what you said but she admitted it. Not that I mind. Now I don't have to have a conscience about what I do.'

'Two wrongs don't make a right, Philip!' Sarah said quietly.

'Maybe not, but I'm human like everyone else. *You* understand these things, don't you, Sarah? You wouldn't blush and turn your face away if I asked you to come to bed with me?'

'Is that a hypothetical question or a suggestion?'

Philip laughed.

'It *was* hypothetical but I'm not going to pretend the thought hasn't entered my mind. Nor yours, I bet. Think about it, Sarah. I think we could enjoy ourselves more than a little.'

He felt for her hand and when she placed it in his, he gave it a gentle squeeze.

'You attract me, Sarah, and I think we'd make quite a pair. Are you shocked at what I'm saying?'

'No, I'm not shocked.' She was, in fact, flattered.

'I'll be back tomorrow afternoon,' he went on. 'You can give me your answer then.'

She knew that the hand he held was trembling. He gave a soft, excited laugh.

'I think I know what your answer is going to be!'

When he left, Sarah went up to her room and lay down on the bed. The pillow felt cool against her hot cheeks.

He wanted her. That mattered; it mattered because she was still smarting from Bill's rebuff and because she knew from her mirror that she was no longer young; soon, perhaps, there would be no more men to desire her.

Other women might manage without sex but she wasn't one of them. Philip knew it instinctively. He didn't think it wrong. He had been the one to say of himself: '*I'm human!*' She had a right to be human, too. And she would not be taking anything away from Noni who was in love with Bill and therefore could not want to be made love to by Philip. There was the time, the opportunity and the place and no reason for her to refuse except that Philip was a married man.

She knew that when tomorrow came, she would not have the strength to say anything else but '*Yes*'!

14

The whole hospital was buzzing with the news that Sarah Bristow had left. No one seemed quite sure where she had gone and Bill was astonished that she had not come to see him before her departure.

For a week, the inevitable rumours circulated. Sarah was secretly married; Sarah was going to have a baby; Sarah had been sacked by Matron; Sarah had been taking drugs. The stories got wilder and wilder and whenever he heard them, Bill tried to stamp on them and discover the truth. Strangely enough, it mattered to him if she were in trouble of some kind. Their lives had crossed and briefly recrossed a second time when he had lost Noni, and Sarah seemed linked in his memory with his love. He could never now ignore the sound of her name, even though he had no personal interest in her, because of her association with the Brisbanes.

He deliberately attended the hospital dance in order to seek out the girl who had been Sarah's friend, Nancy Coutts. But Nancy did not seem to be around anywhere and at last someone informed him that she had left several weeks before to get married. He recalled the wedding then because someone had passed the hat round in the mess for a wedding present for the young doctor she was marrying.

He stood at the bar, watching the dancers and wondering how time, which daily dragged by so slowly, nevertheless had flown past. It was four months since he had last seen Noni. Three months since he had last seen Sarah. Presumably, Philip had left Torquay and was home again. Bill never saw him or Noni in the district.

'Hullo, Aden, how's tricks?'

He turned and raised his glass to the elderly man who had edged in beside him at the bar. It was Herod — the one man who might be able to give him news of the Brisbanes.

'Let me get you a drink, Sir,' he said. He ordered two more whiskies and elbowed a way out of the crush by the bar. Herod mopped his brow and said:

'Never come to these do's as a rule. Not my line.'

'Tell me, Sir, did you ever hear what happened to Philip Brisbane?' Bill was surprised to find his voice so steady. He waited impatiently while the older man took another sip from his glass, mopped his brow a second time. At last he said:

'Didn't you know? He landed a job a couple of months back with B.P.A.S. Someone told me the other day that he'd been invited to do a lecture tour in America. Got to take your hat off to the fellow. Got guts. I thought he'd be a broken man when his career cracked wide open like that.'

'Is he going to America then?' Bill asked.

'Can't tell you. I dare say Harvey might know — he keeps in touch. Brisbane won't speak to me, of course, but I suppose that's only natural. I was the bringer of bad news — and pretty bad at that. He'll always associate me with it, I dare say. That's more your field than mine, eh, Aden?'

Bill did not reply. He had to find out somehow if Noni were going to America. He wasn't sure if he would be glad or sorry if she did. The other side of the world was a very long way away; yet if she were there, he would no longer live with the desperate combination of fear and longing that he might run into her. Whatever he did, wherever he went, his eyes were always looking for her. Again and again, he would see someone who reminded him of her so sharply that it brought a lump to his throat. A neat fair head, a small slim figure, a fur-trimmed suit — always there was some girl who managed to trick his eye-sight for an instant only, but long enough to start his heart beating . . .

' . . . nice little thing, Noni Brisbane!' Bill caught the tail end of Herod's words. 'Often wonder how she put up with Brisbane's particular nature. Not a man who would be easy to live with, I'd say, and probably even less so after the accident.'

'You . . . you've not seen her then?'

'No, though I did run into that nurse, whatshername, the one who's his p.a. now.'

'Nurse? . . . p.a.?' Bill echoed stupidly.

'Yes, you know that red-headed girl. Name like Bishop. I gather she takes Brisbane to his college and helps him in his lectures and generally manages whenever his blindness makes it impossible for him to cope alone. Useful sort of girl. I rather liked her. Nice figure but bad legs!'

'Sarah Bristow helps him with his work? I didn't know.'

'Well, that's what Harvey told me. I gather Brisbane has a flat in town and comes home for weekends. The wife takes over then. I think Harvey went to dinner there a couple of Saturdays past.'

'*I ought not to be surprised!*' Bill thought. But he was. Somehow he had never thought of Sarah going to work for Philip Brisbane. It was just that much too obvious. He ought to have guessed Brisbane liked her, and Sarah had been getting more and more disillusioned with hospital life; she'd wanted a change. No doubt she had jumped at the chance.

And Noni? How did she fit in? She had been the one determined to be Philip's 'right hand man'. Did she go up to London with them or was she alone all week in that house? Was she happy? Lonely? He'd give anything for news of her.

Suddenly he caught sight of Harvey and knew that he had to find out what he could, however odd Harvey thought him for asking. He excused himself and left Herod standing. Harvey nodded as Bill approached.

'Evening, Aden. Glad you younger chaps turn up at these do's. Not dancing?'

'Not at the moment, Sir.' Bill tried to steady his voice. 'I've been having a word with Mr Herod. He was telling me about the job Philip Brisbane landed.'

Harvey grinned.

'Got to hand it to Brisbane. He didn't let much grass grow under his feet, did he? Not only does he pick up a very satisfactory job for himself, but he takes one of our best nurses with him!'

'I gather he is a very determined man!'

'Never really *liked* him, though!' Harvey mumbled with an unusual lack of caution.

231

'Keep that under your hat though, Aden. Talking of determination, there's someone else has a fair share. Do you know that young wife of his taught herself Braille? She can read and type it fluently.'

'Then I imagine she will be going with Brisbane on that American tour?'

'Don't know about that. Brisbane hasn't actually decided whether he'll go or not. But I know his wife is very anxious that he should and that she go with him. When I last saw him, Brisbane was a bit evasive.'

They exchanged a few more comments and Bill got away. He knew he was all kinds of a fool. When Herod had started talking about Sarah being in town with Philip, he'd begun to hope that maybe something might be growing between them — something more than a mere working relationship. But now Harvey had stamped very effectively on such an idea. Noni was striving hard to build up her marriage. She'd not only learned Braille but she was urging Brisbane to take her to America. It could only mean that they were reconciled and that Noni, if she had not actually forgotten him, was building a life without him.

'*It probably wouldn't even bother her if I went to see her,*' he thought bitterly. But he wouldn't go. She'd been happy enough before he entered her life; now she had undoubtedly found the marriage still held something for her and he had no right to unsettle her a second time. Maybe she wouldn't even be unsettled. Maybe their love had never meant as much to her as it had to him. Maybe Philip Brisbane had been right when he'd told Noni that there was no such thing as love; that it was a romantic name people gave to colour more ordinary emotions.

But as he walked out to the car park, feeling the bitter cold of the March wind against his hot face, he knew that love did exist; that it was only love which could cause this heartbreaking sense of loss; this feeling of emptiness, that life had no meaning for him because *she*, his only love, had ceased to care.

★ ★ ★

Noni looked at her husband with eyes widened in disbelief.

'But, Philip, you promised if you went to the States, you would take me. You *promised*!'

Philip turned his head away from the sound of her voice. He felt very much in the wrong and he resented her for being the cause of his discomfort.

'So, I changed my mind!'

Noni sat down heavily in the chair opposite him. Her hands were trembling.

'I worked so very hard at the Braille, Philip. I thought I could help you.'

'I didn't ask you to learn the damned thing!'

Tears sprang to her eyes. She brushed them angrily aside.

'No, you didn't. But I think it only fair you could give me a reason for leaving me behind, Philip. I . . . hoped this trip might be . . . well, a kind of fresh start for us.'

Philip gave a short laugh.

'A second honeymoon? You could hardly say our first was all that much of a success.'

Noni shuddered. Her memories were no happier than Philip's. She had been silly to think that this time everything could be different. Nothing would ever change Philip. She ought to know that by now. Even blindness had not changed him — only changed his work. He had a new career to engross him now. He had not changed.

'I'm very sorry, Noni. I really am!'

She looked up at him, all anger and disappointment gone at the shock of hearing Philip apologize. He had never done such a thing in all their married life. Maybe after all, she had been wrong; he was changing . . .

She went to him and put her hand over his.

'Let's go away together, Philip. I want to be with you — to do things for you. I've never had a chance. With Sarah helping you in London, there's been so little I could do. Please, Philip, take me with you.'

Silence fell between them. Noni thought:

'He'll say yes. He must know now that I'm willing to be a real wife to him — to be everything he wants. We'll have a better chance in new surroundings, away from the past . . .'

'I can't take you. I'm taking Sarah!'

Her hand froze on his. The colour rushed into her cheeks and out again. She stared at him disbelievingly.

'Sarah? But you said you'd take *me*. You said . . . you said it would look bad if Sarah travelled with you alone and . . .'

'You don't understand. I want a divorce!'

She could not take her eyes off his face. He was deliberately trying to turn away from her. He looked quite unlike the Philip she knew; neither arrogant nor angry; almost ashamed . . .

'Well, Noni? Why don't you say something!'

'You want to marry Sarah!'

'As a matter of fact, I do. I'll see you don't suffer financially. I'm sorry to have to hurt you . . . but I've decided it's the only way out. I want Sarah to be with me wherever I go. I need her in my work. I depend upon her absolutely. It's best that I should marry her and then there won't be any difficulty about our being together. I've thought about it very carefully and my mind is quite made up.'

'You're in love with Sarah?'

Now Philip did turn towards the sound of her voice. He was smiling faintly.

'My dear girl, you know I don't believe in love. I'm very fond of Sarah. She's extremely reliable and we get on well. Without meaning to be unpleasant about it, I get along with her a great deal better than I do with you. I'm sorry if that hurts, but it's the truth.'

'And Sarah wants to marry you?'

'I really don't know, I haven't asked her. But I think she will say yes — in fact, I'm sure she will. I know she finds me attractive.'

Noni turned away. She felt an hysterical desire to laugh. The same words coming from anyone else would have been unbelievable. From Philip they were not. What a silly little fool she had been! Struggling here alone day after day to learn Braille so that she could be a good wife to Philip when all the time he and Sarah had been 'getting on well' together in London.

'The divorce,' she said quietly. 'You want me to divorce *you*?'

'That's correct. I can supply you with the

necessary . . . eh, evidence. I . . . I regret to say that on one or two occasions, Sarah and I . . .'

'Don't tell me. I don't want to know. I'll give you a divorce.'

'Well!' said Philip, taking a deep breath. 'I must say you've taken this extremely well, Noni. I thought you might . . . well, cause a bit of a scene. After all, there's a certain amount of loss of face in losing your husband to another woman. However, I dare say people will take into account that Sarah is a nurse and . . . well, I don't think anyone will blame you, Noni!'

Now she was laughing. She could not help it. The tears ran down her cheeks and sobs caught at the laughter, choking her.

'Steady on, my dear!' Philip said anxiously. 'I don't think it's anything to laugh about. I mean, it's a serious matter.'

The laughter and tears stopped as suddenly as they had overtaken her. She stood in the doorway, looking at him, words trembling on her lips. There was so much she might say; could say. How she had given up the very best life had to offer to stand by him; how she had lain awake night after night torn with misery and loneliness and for what . . . *for what?* For a man who, now that he had found someone more advantageous to him in his career, was calmly telling her, his wife, that he had no further use for her.

'Oh, Philip, *poor* Philip!' was all she said, before she left the room to go upstairs and pack a suitcase.

Unaware of her pity and so quite untroubled by it, Philip poured himself a whisky and soda and reached the conclusion that he had handled a very awkward situation very well. But then he had known all along that he could. When he told Sarah about it, she would compliment him. He enjoyed her admiration and he had been a little worried about her reaction to a divorce. Now Noni had offered to step out of the picture, there was no need for any unpleasantness. It did surprise him, on reflection, that Noni hadn't made more of a fuss. She was inclined to be emotional and sentimental and she might have put up a fight to hang on to him. But she had not and now it was nicely fixed. He felt pleased with himself and a little sorry for poor Noni.

★ ★ ★

Bill was in bed, asleep, when the telephone rang. He lifted the receiver and heard a voice say:

'Bill? This is Noni!'

238

He knew he must be dreaming. He switched on the bedside light, and put the receiver to his ear.

'Bill, are you there? This is Noni!' Her voice seemed to be coming from a long way away.

'Noni! Where are you? Oh, darling, Noni darling, where are you?'

There was no reply. He grasped the telephone fiercely and shouted into it.

'Don't go away, Noni, for God's sake, *answer* me. Where are you? Are you at home? Is something wrong?'

'No. I'm all right. I'm not at home. I'm in a call box.'

'Where?'

'At the station. I . . . I was going to Eileen's. Then I thought I couldn't because it was so late so I've been drinking cups of tea in the café. Then I couldn't help it . . . I couldn't stop myself. I *had* to phone you.'

He glanced at his watch and saw that it was eleven-thirty. He said:

'Stay there. I'm coming to get you. Promise me you won't move from there. Promise me, Noni!'

'Bill, I . . . '

'Promise me!'

He dragged on the nearest pair of trousers he could find over his pyjamas, pulled on his overcoat and still in his bedroom slippers, he tore down the stairs. At first his car refused to start. In an agony of impatience, he kept the starter button pressed down and thought that he had choked the engine. Then it coughed and spluttered into life.

He drove the three miles to the station filled with the quite unbearable certainty that when he got there, she would be gone, that he *had* dreamed the whole crazy conversation and she had never phoned at all; that he was beginning to have hallucinations and, like one of his patients, had tricked himself into believing what he wanted to believe in order to make himself happy.

She was standing outside the phone box, her fair hair blowing across her face. He braked sharply, jumped out of the car and ran to her.

As he held her in his arms, he could feel the trembling of her body through the thickness of both their coats.

'My God, you're frozen,' he said, and took off his own coat to put round her. Her eyes were shining, but not with tears.

'Bill, darling, you can't — you're wearing pyjamas!'

He grinned happily.

'And a fat lot I care. Jump in, darling.'

He cradled her close against him all the

way home. He had a thousand questions to ask her but the fact of having her there, close against him, her head heavy on his shoulder, was stirring him to such deep emotions he couldn't speak. Noni, too, was silent.

He led her upstairs and into his flat, his arm still held tightly around her. He left her to switch on the electric fire. When he turned, she was staring at him from eyes which suddenly seemed far too big in her pale, serious face.

'You've lost weight!' He went across to her and lifted his overcoat from her shoulders. 'Darling, will you have to go? Can you stay?'

She answered at once but the second seemed an eternity before she said:

'I can stay, Bill, if you want me.'

'If!' He was filled with an incredible excitement. He hurried into the bedroom and returned with a big blue blanket which he wrapped around her. Then he went back for his dressing gown. Next he went to the sideboard and poured out a glass of brandy; he stood watching her while she obediently drank it. Some colour came back into her cheeks. She looked at him, a smile beginning in the depths of her eyes and at the corners of her mouth.

'Noni!'

As he took her in his arms, he knew that

whatever had happened or might happen, he could *never* let her go again. Even if it should prove unfair to Philip, bad for Noni, wrong in the eyes of the world, he simply could not let her go. He would fight everything and everyone to keep her.

He kissed her so fiercely that she pulled away from him, eyes shining, and gently touched his cheek with her hand. He caught hold of it and held it there, his eyes closed against the pain of remembering the last time she had done that.

'Tell me,' he whispered. 'How long have I got you for?'

'Let me go and I'll tell you!' she said softly between his kisses. 'I . . . can't . . . speak . . . when you . . . '

But he could not stop kissing her.

'One for every day we've been parted!' he said hungrily. 'One for each kiss I've given you in my thoughts. One for every kiss I may not be able to give you in the future.'

But he stopped kissing her suddenly and said:

'Noni, *how long have we got?*'

Holding hands, she told him; about Philip's request for a divorce, about Sarah, about the failure of all her efforts to be the right wife for Philip.

He looked at her aghast.

'And when you knew you could have your freedom, you decided to go to your *sister*?'

'Oh, darling!' She kissed him quickly and fiercely. 'I wasn't sure if *you* still wanted me. It's been months since I saw you or spoke to you. I thought perhaps you'd found someone else; that maybe I'd just imagined you loved me because your love meant so much to me. I dared not believe in it in case it wasn't so. I was going to wait until you found out — someone in the hospital would have told you — wait and see if you came to find me.'

'Noni, you silly little idiot. You might have wasted weeks . . . my God, I can't bear to think about it. You knew why I didn't get in touch with you. It was what you wanted. But for that I could never have kept away from you. I love you, darling, I love you.'

She smiled tremulously.

'Yes, I know! But I'm afraid, Bill. I failed Philip . . . I didn't make him a good wife. Maybe . . . '

'You didn't fail him, Noni. He just didn't need you. I do. You did everything humanly possible to make your marriage work. You cannot blame yourself now.'

'But if you and I hadn't fallen in love . . . '

He put a finger over her lips.

'No, dearest Noni. Your marriage to Philip had failed before we ever met. It never was a marriage really, was it?'

She shook her head.

'I suppose not. We were just two people living together. Oh, Bill, do you think he'll be happy with Sarah? I don't want him to be unhappy.'

'I'm sure Philip will always get what he wants out of life. He has probably chosen just the right person for him. Sarah is no fool . . . she must know what he has to offer and the limitations, as well as the advantages. If she marries him, she'll give him what he wants and take what she wants. They are two of a kind.'

Noni drew a deep sigh.

'Then we don't need to have a conscience about them? We can be happy together?'

'My darling, yes! We will be very, *very* happy together.'

It was the moment in his life when everything in the world he wanted was his at last, his in a way he had not dared to dream of. Noni was free and she had come to him. She loved him and there was no one in the world to prevent them from giving the fullest expression to their love. But he knew that, whatever the iron control he must needs exert, he must not make love to her tonight. Tomorrow he would drive her down to her sister and there he would visit her, write to her, telephone her, but never touch her.

He tried to find the right words to explain it to her. It was as if a miracle had happened and they had been given the most precious gift of all, a new life, a second chance. This time everything must be perfect. No one would have the right to point a finger at them, to condemn them; no one would ever be able to make Noni feel that a single particle of their relationship was wrong or bad. It might be a long time before the divorce was finally accomplished, but they would wait until he could really call Noni his wife.

'I want it to be quite, quite perfect, Noni. Do you understand, darling? Do you?'

Noni looked at him wonderingly. This was Bill, the man she loved more than life itself, the man she was going to marry. She had not thought ahead as he had, but now that she heard him explaining what it was he wanted for them, she knew that, as always, he had chosen the very path she herself most wanted. Perhaps it would not always be like this; perhaps there would be times when they even quarrelled or took opposite views. But she knew with a sudden and complete certainty that in the big things, the things that really mattered, Bill and she were not two people, because they thought as one.

'I didn't know it was possible to be so

245

happy, or so much in love!' she said softly.

'Or so hungry?'

'Or so hungry!'

'Bacon . . .'

'And eggs!'

They laughed simultaneously and went out to Bill's kitchen, their hands like their thoughts and their hearts, closely linked.

THE END

TIME AFTER TIME
AND OTHER STORIES

Mary Williams

In this collection of mysterious short stories the recurring theme of 'time after time' is reflected upon with varying intensity, and in several as a haunting reminder of life's immortality. Time itself has little meaning in the wheel of eternity, and it is more than possible that the vital spark or soul of any human being could by chance contact that of another known to him or her in a previous existence on earth. Some stories concentrate on the effect of wandering apparitions about the ether and in all of them can be found love, tragedy, emotional yearnings and sheer terror.

DEAD FISH

Ruth Carrington

Dr Geoffrey Quinn arrives home to find his children missing, the charred remains of his wife's body in the boiler and Chief Superintendent Manning waiting to arrest him for her murder. Alison Hope, attractive and determined, is briefed to defend him. Quinn claims he is innocent, but Alison is not so sure. The background becomes increasingly murky as she penetrates a wealthy and ruthless circle who cannot risk their secrets — sexual perversion, drugs, blackmail, illegal arms dealing and major fraud — coming to light. Can Alison unravel the mystery in time to save Quinn?

MY FATHER'S HOUSE

Kathleen Conlon

'Your father has another woman'. Nine-year-old Anna Blake is only mildly surprised when a schoolfriend lets drop this piece of information. And when her father finally leaves home to live with Olivia in Hampstead, that place becomes, for Anna, the epitome of sinful glamour. But Hampstead, though welcoming, is not home. So Anna, now in her teens, sets out to find a place where she can really belong. At first she thinks love may be the answer, and certainly Jonathon — and Raymond — and Jake, have a devastating effect on her life. But can anyone really supply what she needs?